FALLING FOR A FABLE

Mustang Cross Book One

Karryn Overstreet

To my parents who supported my dream of being an author.

AUTHOR'S NOTE

When I wrote this story, I knew I wanted the heroine Sharona to have a troubled background. However, I've aimed to balance the heavy past of her character with this lighthearted story and the sweet hero who gives her a home.

As someone who prefers low angst in stories, I've tried to handle the topics listed on the Content Warning page as delicately as possible. I've also given a few more details on that page, so you, the reader, can be aware of the scope of the sensitive topics. Please be mindful when reading. Rest assured that this book ends in a happily ever after.

CONTENT WARNING

· · ● ● · ● ● ● · ·

This story is a sweet romance that touches on the below sensitive topics:

Abuse (physical and verbal; mentioned but not graphic)

Alcohol usage and abuse (mentioned but not graphic)

Attempted sexual assault (past incident mentioned briefly and no descriptive details given)

Cheating (mentioned but not committed by the main hero or heroine)

Death of a loved one (moderately referenced throughout book)

Language (explicit language is implied or cut off in a few places; the word *crap* is used in Chapter 27, for those who need more details)

Murder of a loved one (mentioned but no descriptive details given)

Substance abuse (moderately referenced throughout book)

Trauma (moderately referenced throughout book)

SHARONA'S RULES

• • • ● ● ● ● ● • • •

1. Never fall in love.

2. Stay away from drugs.

3. Never be alone with one of Mom's boyfriends.

4. Cooking can save my life.

5. All I need in life is money.

6. Peanut butter sandwiches are my friend.

7. We only trust each other. If I'm ever in trouble, call Saint.

8. Go with my gut.

9. Family business is for family.

CHAPTER I

· · · ● ●· ● ● ● · ·

SHARONA

As a girl born on October thirty-first, I expected my nineteenth birthday to go like many of the others. Cheap gifts, a cake I made myself, or maybe no acknowledgment at all.

But tonight has propelled itself to the top of my list of bad birthdays.

The lampposts overhead shine their light on my path. I shuffle along the deserted street, grateful for the past hour of solitude. If I walk a little bit further, I'll reach the diner toward the outskirts of town. I may be new to Mustang Cross, but I remember passing the restaurant when we arrived six days ago. Maybe they'll have a back room where I can stay the night.

All the shops in this town are closed by now, but I hold onto hope. Hope for a late-night kindness.

I huddle into Saint's leather jacket, his memory giving me strength.

Rule Eight: Go with my gut.

The rule repeats over and over in my head. It's the only rule I can cling to in this moment. Rule seven will never help me again, and rule three broke a few hours ago.

Saint's voice fills my mind. *Go with your gut, Sharona. If you feel like you need to run, come find me. We'll run together.*

But he's not here.

The night air cools my bare legs. My earlier panic drove me into choosing flip-flops and cut-off shorts before I crept out of my bedroom window. But I welcome the break from the south Texas humidity. The change in the weather feels like a promise from Saint as I run from my home.

No. It's a new *house*. I don't have a home.

Lights from the Hog Heaven diner burst through the darkness like a lighthouse guiding me to safety. I heft my duffel bag further up my shoulder as I approach the front door. The lights inside illuminate the empty booths and tables. But someone has to be here. Diners stay open past ten, right?

When I pull on the handle, the door remains shut. Locked.

I jiggle the handle. "Hello?" I bang on the glass door. "Hello!" Please, don't be closed.

A man in his mid-thirties walks through a set of swinging doors into the dining area.

My body stiffens. Maybe I didn't think this through.

Another man with a missing forearm shoulders past him. My stomach curdles. After what happened a few hours ago, I don't want to be anywhere near a man, let alone two.

They walk my way, and I flee in the direction I came.

Or I try.

My foot slips out of my flip-flop, and I stumble. I land on my stuffed duffel which ends up sandwiched between my stomach and the ground. The asphalt digs into my palms as I push to my feet. With my duffel bag situated once again on my shoulder and my shoe secure on my foot, I gear up for a more composed flight away from the diner.

"Wait! Hey! Come back!"

I freeze at the sound of a woman's voice. My muscles bunch as I turn to the diner's entrance.

A young brunette woman pushes both of the men. "Get out of my way."

The blond guy throws his arm in front of her like a shield. "Ally, stop."

"*You* stop," she says. "You're making her nervous." She manages to squeeze in between them. "Hi. Can we help you?"

My gaze jumps between the three strangers.

The woman wiggles her fingers in a small wave. "I'm Allegra."

My fingers clench around my shoulder strap. "Sh-Sharona."

"Nice to meet you."

The man with brown hair crosses his muscular arms. "The kitchen isn't open right now, but you can come back in the morning."

Allegra elbows him. "Grady, a sandwich wouldn't be hard to make."

"I don't want food," I say. "Just a place to stay the night."

The blond man's gaze skims over my face, I guess taking in the bruises on my skin. "We don't want any trouble."

"Neither do I." Tears sting my eyes at the thought of what happened earlier. "Please. I need help. Just for tonight."

"Of course," Allegra says. "There's a bed and breakfast that opened up two years ago." She looks at either of the guys. "Do one of y'all want to take her to Diane's?"

I take a step back. "It's okay. I can walk there, if you point me in the right direction."

Her eyes narrow on me before she beams at the blond man next to her. "Why don't you go with me and Kip? We can leave Grady to lock up."

The other man—Grady—throws his hands up in the air. "I didn't need you here in the first place."

Allegra whirls on him.

The blond man touches her arm. "Ally, we need to get home."

Her glare remains fixed on Grady before she gestures toward a side street. "We're parked around back, if you want to follow us."

She takes off with the blond man, Kip. Grady walks back inside, and I follow the other two around the diner. I prefer a ride with her and Kip than with both of the men.

We arrive at the bed and breakfast in under two minutes. I climb out of the back seat with my bag of possessions. After shutting the door, I trail after Kip and Allegra toward the small remodeled two-story house. White trim compliments the blue siding, and two rocking chairs sit on a cute porch facing the street. A sign stands in the front yard with the name *McKellar Inn*.

Allegra opens the door. "Knock, knock!"

I follow her into the inn and step away from Kip who's right behind me.

A young woman with golden hair stands at a small receptionist desk.

Allegra gives her a smile. "Genevieve! I didn't know you were back."

She circles the desk and hugs Allegra. "I just arrived a few hours ago."

"And Diane has you working already?"

"I don't mind. I love it here. But y'all are out late for a weeknight. Where are the kids?"

"They're with Kip's parents. I had to help Grady with something at the diner."

Kip scoffs and slides next to Allegra. "More like she wanted to boss Grady around."

Allegra gestures to me. "This is Sharona. She showed up at the diner looking for a place to stay the night."

The blond woman extends her hand. "Hi, I'm Genevieve. I'm helping manage the McKellar Inn for the next few weeks. It's nice to meet you."

I give her hand a quick shake. "You too."

Allegra slaps the top of the desk. "Well, I'll leave y'all to it."

Kip opens the front door for her, and she brushes past me.

She stops and looks at me over her shoulder. "If you need anything, just stop by the diner. I'm usually there." She wishes us a good night and leaves with Kip.

Genevieve returns to the other side of the desk. "Now, let's see here." She flips through the papers in front of her. "You only need one night?"

"Maybe."

Her eyes scan me like I'm a dissected fish, taking in my attire and belongings. "You're just passing through?"

I'm not sure what I'm doing actually. "I moved here a few days ago with—" I shift on my feet. "To a house about two miles from town, but I'm... I might be looking for a different place."

"Well, we have very reasonable prices, and we do have a room available. Come next week, though, we're doing some renovations." Her face scrunches. "Termites. They've done a number on a few of the rooms. We'll be closed for a while, so we can do the repairs." She writes on a piece of paper. "So one night or two?"

Who am I kidding? If I could live here permanently, it would help.

I fidget with my duffel's strap. "Maybe two."

"Two nights will be two hundred."

My stomach drops at her words. That's almost all the cash I have in my purse. "Actually, I'll just do one night."

"Are you sure?"

"Yes."

She stares at me and taps her pen against the desk. "I'll mark you down for two nights."

"I can't afford it."

"I'll talk to Diane. I'm sure she won't mind." She searches through a drawer and removes a key. "She owns McKellar Inn and should be here tomorrow. Let me show you to your room."

I have a place to stay. For free. That knowledge chips away at the weight of the past few hours. Saint must be watching over me.

Genevieve leads me down the hall and opens the door of a bedroom. "I'll put you by the bathroom, so you don't have to go wandering around trying to find it."

She flicks on the light switch, illuminating the small room. The white walls contrast with the dark wooden furniture. A bed rests against the side wall, the comforter a swirl of light blue and white. The neatness and cleanliness roll over me like waves and calm the storm inside me.

I drop my stuff onto the floor by the desk. "This is perfect. Thank you."

Genevieve holds the key out to me. "I'm staying in the house behind the inn, if you need anything."

As soon as she leaves, I lock the door. I take a seat on the bed and shrug out of Saint's jacket.

My fingers glide over the soft material. I lift the leather to my nose, willing the scent of my brother's spicy cologne to form, but it's long gone. A lump forms in my throat as I step to the desk. I drape Saint's jacket over the chair and pat the smooth leather.

After I change into my pajamas, I turn off the light and settle under the covers. I take a deep breath and close my eyes. Saint's smiling face fills my mind, an anchor when I desperately need his comfort.

And his voice once again seems so close.

Happy birthday, Sharona.

CHAPTER 2

•••••••••••

SHARONA

MY BODY ACHES THE next morning from my injuries and all the walking last night. But even though I'm sore and I tossed and turned all night, I slept better than I have in months.

As I crawl out of bed, I wince at the sore spot on my side. I grab the hand mirror from my duffel and check my face. Two small bruises bloom on my cheek and along my jaw. My bottom lip has a small cut on the right side, but it's stopped bleeding. When I lift my sleeve, bruises in the shape of fingers decorate my upper arm.

Images from last night rush through my mind. I squeeze my eyes shut, wishing memories were as easy to wipe away as my tears.

After collecting myself, I search for my phone charger but stop with the cord in my hand. What's the point of a full battery if I have nobody I want to call?

I power down my phone and toss it on top of the turned-out duffel.

What am I going to do? I have three hundred bucks to my name, no job, no permanent place to stay, and nobody to count on.

The jacket hanging on the desk chair lures me closer, and I fiddle with the collar. "I wish you were with me, Saint. We'd find a new home."

My stomach rumbles, and I change into a T-shirt and jeans and slip out of the room. When I find the kitchen, the lights are off, but the sun shines through the small windows of a door on the opposite side of the room. The clean appliances and organized shelves calm me with their ordered state. Everything has its place, unlike the piles of dishes and crowded counters in my mom's house.

I'm not sure if I'm allowed to use the kitchen, but the rumbling in my stomach convinces me to search for food. I wash my hands and find ingredients for toast, eggs, and bacon. While I gather the necessary utensils to make my breakfast, rule four floats to the front of my mind.

Cooking can save my life.

Since our mother often left us alone, Saint and I taught ourselves how to cook. At first, we cooked out of necessity. But it became another flicker of joy that brought light into our dark lives.

As I set a skillet on one of the burners on the stove, the door to the kitchen opens. I grab a knife nearby and spin around, ready to fight any unwanted guests.

Genevieve steps inside and shuts the door. With her black pants, burgundy top, and heels, she looks ready for a business meeting rather than a day at a small inn with one lonely guest. Her hair flows down her back in smooth waves, reminding me I forgot to brush my own.

"Good morning." She glances at the skillet then at me. "I was just coming to make you breakfast, but it looks like you got it covered."

I place the knife on the counter, hoping she ignores my attack position. "I'm sorry for helping myself to the food."

"No need to apologize. Why don't you crack the eggs, and I'll start on the bacon."

We work in comfortable silence, cooking eggs, bacon, and toast. The meal may be simple, but it beats my quick dinner last night of canned soup and crackers. The aroma of sizzling pork permeates the kitchen, and my stomach growls again.

I touch my belly, willing it to stop embarrassing me. "Sorry."

Genevieve laughs and grabs two plates from a cupboard. "I'm the one who's sorry. Some hostess I was. I should have fed you last night. Did you eat dinner?"

"Yes, but... it was small."

Her eyes narrow, but as if I imagined it, she's smiling once again. "Coffee?"

"No thanks." I don't need coffee. My brain is wide awake from the nightmares of my reality.

After she plates our food, we move to the dining room. She sits at the head of the table, and I take the seat next to her.

She folds her hands. "Do you mind if I pray for our food?"

I fidget with my fork. "No, go ahead."

She bows her head and prays aloud. I stare at my food, not knowing what to do.

I've only prayed one time in my life—the morning I found out about Saint. I prayed for it to be a dream, but it was real. I hoped if I prayed hard enough and long enough everything would be fixed.

But Saint was gone, and I learned prayer doesn't help.

Genevieve ends her prayer and picks up her fork. "Any plans for today?"

I stab my eggs. "I hadn't really thought about it."

"You can hang out around the inn. Diane gave me a list to do, so I'll be around."

"I can help, if you need it. To say thank you for letting me stay here."

"You don't have to do that."

"But I want to. I can help with cooking, especially since it's just us. And I can clean. Anything to help."

She gives me a soft smile. "Thank you. I would appreciate it."

The front door opens and slams shut.

"Diane!" a man calls. "You never answered me about the popcorn you wanted." His voice thunders down the hall, the slow thud of boots growing louder.

The man steps into the small space with a cowboy hat clutched in his hand. A scowl etches his face, and I flinch, prepared to receive a man's temper.

His frown shifts from me to my hostess. "Genevieve?"

She scrambles to her feet. "Tex. Hi."

"What are you doing here?"

"I'm in town for the remodeling. Diane's letting me stay in the house out back for now."

His eyes slide down her body before flicking back to her face. "It's been awhile."

"About two years."

My back slouches against my chair as Genevieve stares at the man. She seems fine with him. At least he's not yelling anymore.

He glances at me and clears his throat. "Sorry if I'm interrupting. I didn't know you had company."

Genevieve pats my shoulder. "This is Sharona. She's staying for a few days."

He dips his head in my direction. "Tex Honeycutt. Nice to meet you, Sharona."

"You, too," I say from my seat.

Genevieve gestures to the food. "She helped me cook this morning. Would you like something to eat?"

"I'm in a bit of a rush," Tex says. "I have a long morning at the store, so I can help Isobel at the farm later. She said they might need to replace some of the posts on the porch, and they wanted my opinion."

Genevieve presses her lips together. "They do need extra help, don't they? I've been talking to Blake. Maybe someone could help with the cooking and cleaning."

Tex's gaze flashes to me before swinging back to her. "I know what you're thinking, and I don't think it's a good idea. They're a tight-knit bunch."

"I know, but they could use her."

My pulse spikes at her words, but at this point, anything has to be an improvement over my current situation.

I stand. "Are y'all talking about a job?"

Tex runs his hand through his hair. "Not really. They wouldn't be able to pay you."

"But you could partake of the meals you cook," Genevieve says. "You wouldn't have to pay for food."

That would be one less expense to worry about. I could have food to eat and a place to stay while saving my money. At least for a couple more days.

Genevieve grins. "They could start by cooking with you and overseeing you until they think you can make the meals on your own. Is that something you think you would enjoy?"

Would I like eating for free? Would I like spending my time cooking instead of worrying about someone finding out where I am?

"Yes," I say.

Tex looks at my gracious hostess. "I'll give them a call." His gaze finds mine. "If they say yes, you can start your new job today."

CHAPTER 3

· · · · ● · ● · · · ·

RYKER

WHEN I CLIMB OFF the seat for the lawnmower, my cellphone rings. I pull it out of my pocket and answer the incoming call from Tex. "Yeah?"

"Hey, Ryker. Sorry to bug you while you're working."

"No, it's fine. What's up?"

"I just stopped at Diane's." He clears his throat. "There's a girl here. She says she wants a job. I know y'all were trying to find some help since..."

He leaves me to fill in the well-known blanks. That betrayal is still raw for us all.

"Anyway," he says, "I don't know who she is, but she can cook. I thought y'all might be able to use her help around the house. Maybe do a trial run at first. But it's your call." He pauses. "She's got bruises on her, and she looks as skittish as a deer in the middle of huntin' season. I think she's running from something."

I blow out a breath and plop onto the seat of the mower. My first instinct is to say no to inviting strangers onto our property. This girl could be a thief or unstable.

But we really need the help. She could work around the house while we maintain the farm. From the sound of it, she needs a job as much as we could use an extra set of hands.

"Okay, I'll ask the others."

"Let me know," he says before he hangs up.

My eyes drift to the cows in the pasture. To the henhouse a few yards away. To the fields farther back, ready for the fall harvest.

My family started Fable Farms years ago. We've grown from a family farm to a thriving business. I've worked hard to build our reputation with the help of my friends.

A thousand acres under my family's name, but Fable Farms is home to many. Whatever we decide about the farm—including hiring this new girl—we do it with the support of everyone.

I open the text thread labeled Farm Fam.

Ryker:

> Family meeting at the main house. Now.

Blake:

> What's wrong?

Kieran:

> Can't. Busy.

Ryker:

> Tex called. He wants to bring someone to help us on the farm.

Isobel:

> Why didn't my dad call me?

> Never mind. He's calling me now.

Stephen:

> Heading to the main house, but I can't stay long. I need to pick up Boaz.

Blake:

> On my way to the house.

Kieran:

> Fine, I'm coming too. But I think you could handle the hire without me.

Ryker:

> She wouldn't help on the farm. Tex thought she'd help with cooking.

Stephen:

> She?

Isobel:

> I'm on my way. My dad gave me a recapitulation.

Kieran:

> Just say recap. Stop using big words just because you can.

Isobel:

> Do you mean having a vocabulary? Something you lack?

I roll my eyes and pocket my phone. Though it's entertaining, I don't have time for their banter today.

Blake Montgomery, the farm's foreman, arrives first and meets me at the porch steps.

He leans against the bottom post. "How'd Tex find this woman?"

"I don't want to repeat myself. Let's wait for the others."

My friend Stephen parks one of the four-wheelers outside the barn and heads our way. Our other friends Isobel and Kieran join us a few minutes later.

Kieran points a calf bottle at me. "You made me leave in the middle of feeding my baby. She's bellering for her bottle."

One of our cows had twins, and we've had to bottle-feed the smaller of the calves for the past two weeks. Or I should say, Kieran has had to bottle-feed it. He's got a soft spot for the calves.

I cross my arms. "This won't take long. Tex said there's a girl staying at the inn who might be able to help us."

Stephen frowns. "Does she know we can't pay her?"

"I don't know, but we've been struggling without Alessandro." With the reminder of the tragedy we faced this year, I steer clear of discussing the other problem we've had these past few months. "We need more help. She could maintain the house and do the cooking, so we don't have to worry about it."

Kieran cocks his head. "This girl, who we don't know, would cook our food and spend time alone in our house?"

"She showed up at Diane's last night with bruises. Tex said she looks scared more than anything."

Blake rubs the back of his neck. "Yeah, my sister shot me a text about her."

"I can't knowingly turn her away," I say. "Not if she needs help."

Kieran props his hand on his hip. "You can't possibly be thinking about eating anything she makes. She could poison it or something."

"How would she even do that?" Blake asks.

"There are multiple ways," Kieran says. "All she has to do is look online."

Stephen nudges him. "It sounds like she has bigger problems on her plate than thinking about clever ways to murder us."

Kieran glares. "What about rifling through our stuff? She could be a thief."

I lift my hand. "One of us will be with her whenever she's here."

Isobel nods. "From what my dad told me, it looks like she comes from a bad situation."

"Genevieve thinks the kid needs help," Blake says.

Stephen's eyes widen. "Kid? How old is she?"

"Genevieve didn't know, but she said she looks young. I think we should give her a chance."

"I vote yes," Isobel says.

"Me, too," I say.

Stephen grins at Kieran. "I cast my vote with the majority. What do you think, Hennessy?"

Kieran lifts his finger. "Fine, but eyes on her the whole time she's here."

I type a message to Tex.

Ryker:

The fam says bring her. Say around lunch?

Tex:

I'll let Genevieve know.

I pocket my phone. "Genevieve's bringing her later. We'll each help with the cooking—"

"Except for Kieran," Isobel says. "Now, that'll kill you."

He shoots her a scowl. "Love you, too."

I ignore them. "We'll each take turns cooking meals with her, so she's not alone. I'll start her off today."

Blake pushes off the porch railing. "Sounds good. Let us know when lunch is ready."

Everyone returns to their daily chores, and I take a seat on the lawnmower. What if this girl tries to steal something? What if she tries to hurt one of us? Can I trust her in my house? With my family?

Questions and scenarios run through my mind as I start the lawnmower back up. After what we've been through, I can only hope this girl doesn't create more problems for us.

Genevieve Montgomery's tan hatchback appears on our private road. Our blue heeler, Blue, chases the car and tries to bite the tires. I whistle at him as I walk down the porch steps. He scampers to the house as Genevieve parks her car.

She gets out and rounds the hood to the passenger side. "Hey, Ryker. Thanks for doing this."

"No problem."

A young girl climbs out and stands next to Genevieve. She has to be a few years younger than me, perhaps still in high school. Her eyes dart from me to her surroundings, the quick movements increasing as she walks my way with Genevieve. When they reach me, I catch the cut on her lip and the bruises on her skin.

Tex wasn't lying. She screams trouble.

Genevieve places her hand on the girl's arm. "This is Sharona. Tex said he talked to you about us stopping by."

I extend my hand. "Ryker Fable. It's nice to meet you."

The girl hesitates and slips her hand in mine. She barely shakes it before pulling her arm closer to her.

"Thanks," I say to Genevieve. "I'll take it from here."

She turns to Sharona. "You're in good hands. These are some of the best men in town."

The young brunette flinches and backs away with wide eyes.

Genevieve meets my gaze and lifts her eyebrows to signal me. "Actually, maybe I'll stay for a bit. If that's okay with you, Ryker."

"Sure." Because I can't say no. Sharona clearly retreated at the thought of being alone with me. "Welcome to Fable Farms."

She glances down, her hair shifting to cover part of her face.

This is going to be new. I've grown up around Isobel and my little sister Tinka along with plenty of other women in this town who speak their minds. Even the quiet girls aren't this withdrawn.

I jerk my thumb over my shoulder. "Let's head inside and get started."

They follow me into the house, and Genevieve whispers to Sharona. I lead them down the hall without a backward glance though I'm tempted to pry some words out of the newcomer.

Once we're settled in the kitchen, I lean against the counter. "Here's our situation. We've been struggling for a couple months, so we could use any help we can get. One of our farmhands passed recently and another..." I shake my head and bypass discussing that situation further. "Did Genevieve or Tex tell you we're going to test this arrangement out for a few days?"

Sharona nods. "Yes."

Her voice springs up like the honeysuckle that grows on our trees. Fresh, delicate. Sweet.

Genevieve takes a seat at the small table in the center of the kitchen. "And I told her y'all couldn't pay her, but her payment would be partaking in the meals with y'all."

I wash my hands in the sink. "We mostly make sandwiches for lunch and save the cooking for dinner." I open the cupboard and pull out ingredients for pancakes. "Since we're trying to figure out if we're a good fit for each other, we'll be doing as much cooking as we can in the afternoon. Sound good?"

After a beat, Sharona shuffles over to the sink to wash her hands. "Yes."

Same word, same soft edge.

I hold up the bag of flour. "My specialty is breakfast, so we're doing pancakes for lunch."

When her brown eyes focus on me, something inside me shifts. I once again catalog the small bruises on her face. Who would be cruel enough to hurt this girl?

She steps to my side. "How can I help?"

We cook breakfast for lunch like a well-oiled machine. By the time we're flipping the pancakes, Sharona moves around the kitchen like it's her own. I prop myself against the counter, letting her take the wheel. Genevieve gives me a wink, and I smile.

Sharona rifles through the cupboard and pulls out the cinnamon. She sprinkles the spice on top of the pancakes cooking on the griddle.

"Do you normally add cinnamon to pancakes?" I ask.

She jerks and drops the container of cinnamon. It bounces off the counter and falls to the floor. Unfortunately, she had taken the lid off. A rust-colored cloud wafts from the linoleum as cinnamon splatters everywhere.

She gasps and backs away from the mess. "I'm sorry. I'll clean it up right away. It won't happen again."

When I lift my hand to reassure her, she flinches.

As if she anticipates that I'm about to hit her.

I drop my hand. "Sharona, it's fine."

"No, I'm sorry. I should have asked you about the cinnamon. And then I dropped it on the floor."

"Sharona—"

She dashes out of the kitchen, and Genevieve gets to her feet.

I hold up my hand. "I'll get her. If this is going to work, she has to learn I won't hurt her."

She frowns but nods.

The screen door slams shut at the front of the house. I take off down the hall, wondering why I want to convince this girl I'm not a threat. All I know is I don't like how Sharona shies away from people. Especially me.

CHAPTER 4

· · · ● · ● · ● · ·

SHARONA

I MESSED UP.

He's going to be angry.

Run away.

Those thoughts circle my mind as I bolt down the porch steps. My head swivels from side to side.

Where do I go? What do I do?

The red barn a few yards away would be a good hiding place, but the people on this farm will search for me. The dirt road would eventually lead me back to town, but that would mean more walking than I did last night. My sore body screams in protest.

The door shuts behind me, and I whirl around.

Ryker raises his hands. "I'm going to stay right here. All I want to do is talk."

"I'm sorry. Please. I'm sorry."

"What are you sorry for?"

"I should have asked you about the cinnamon."

"You didn't have to ask. I'm sure it'll be delicious."

He seems genuine, but I've learned sometimes you have to watch out for the kind ones.

"But I spilled it," I say. "I made a huge mess."

He shrugs. "Accidents happen."

"I'll clean it up, I promise."

"And I'll help. We'll get it cleaned up in no time."

I take a step back. This must be a trick.

True to his word, he stays where he is on the porch. "I'm not angry, Sharona."

How can he not be? At my mom's house, I would have earned a reprimand for my incompetence or clumsiness. Men criticize. They take control and assume authority over any woman. Especially when she's wrong.

Ryker's gaze remains fixed on mine. "Would you like to leave? I can tell Genevieve you're done for the day, if you don't want to finish the meal."

My eyes narrow. "You'd let me leave."

"Yes."

One hour at this place has thrown me into confusion. Men take what they want with no regard for a woman's feelings. But Ryker doesn't pressure me. Instead, he's willing to keep his distance even when I didn't ask. Like what I want matters.

My shoulders drop. "I'm sorry."

"You don't have to apologize. It's fine. Let's go finish those pancakes, yeah?"

"Okay."

A smile spreads across his face. "And we'll add cinnamon to a few of them. I'm sure the others will love them."

We walk back into the house, and Genevieve stands at the other end of the hall with a frown. I give her a nod to let her know I'm fine, and her frown disappears. Ryker helps me clean up the mess before we turn our attention back to the meal. He and Genevieve keep an easy conversation going as we plate the pancakes and scramble the eggs.

"I'll get the others," Ryker says, after the food is on the table in the dining room.

He returns to the kitchen, and I peek into the small room. After he opens a side door leading outside, he grabs a metal spoon and strikes it against a large triangle dangling from a small overhang.

Every clang reverberates within me, spiking my pulse. He said others. How many others are on the farm? And how many of them are men?

I shift closer to Genevieve, her presence and steady gaze calming me.

The front door opens and shuts. Boots clomp against the wood floor, and I spin around to face the hallway.

A tall cowboy wearing a flashy belt buckle reaches the dining room. He holds the hand of a little boy who can't be more than two. The man looks a few years older than me, maybe the same age as Ryker.

He places his cowboy hat on a hook and runs his fingers through his curly black hair. "Hi there. I'm Stephen Santos. You must be Sharona."

"Yes. Nice to meet you."

"It's my pleasure." He jostles the little boy's arm. "And this handsome fella is my son Boaz."

"Hi, Boaz."

He rushes forward and wraps his arms around my legs.

Stephen laughs as he pulls his son back toward him. "Sorry. He's a ladies' man." He glances at Ryker. "How did lunch go?"

"Sharona did a great job," he says.

"Sounds great."

The front door opens again. Someone else walks through the kitchen door, and more people file into the dining room.

I take a step toward Genevieve, but she walks to a blond man who appears in the threshold.

He gives her a hug. "I would've come in sooner to say hi if I'd known you were still here."

"I didn't want to pull you away from work," she says. "I was fine helping Sharona and Ryker in the kitchen."

Though she just sat in the chair because I was too much of a chicken to be alone with a guy.

She steps to my side and gestures to the man. "Sharona, this is my brother Blake." She indicates a woman with hair the color of caramel. "This is Isobel. And that's Kieran."

The last man scowls at me.

I shrink away from him. "Nice to meet y'all."

Kieran walks into the kitchen as the others file around the table.

"Is this mine?" Stephen takes a sip out of a glass of orange juice.

"It is now," Isobel says. "Nobody wants your germs."

"Thanks, Is."

The refrigerator door slams shut.

Kieran storms back into the room and advances toward me. "Did you touch my stash?"

I stumble back. "No, I don't know—I didn't touch anything."

Ryker claps his friend on the shoulder. "Chill. I put your jam on the counter."

Isobel sighs. "Stop being so grumpy."

The redheaded man looks over his shoulder into the kitchen. My mind sprints to find a solution to please the angry man.

"I think you owe Sharona an apology," Blake says.

I shake my head, hoping to unruffle Kieran's feathers. "No, it's fine."

"Sorry," Kieran says. "I shouldn't have lost my cool like that."

"It's fine." Just get him away from me, please.

Ryker slides closer to me. "Why don't you have a seat?"

Blake and Kieran leave the room as I take the seat next to Genevieve. Blake returns with another chair, and Kieran walks back into the room holding a jar of jelly.

Ryker clears his throat. "Sharona, we say grace at every meal."

"That's fine."

"We usually hold hands."

My eyes widen.

He lifts his hand. "We're not expecting you to do it. I just wanted you to know."

They all hold hands, and I fold my own in my lap. Prayer number two for today. Do these people pray all day? And do they believe it helps? But I'd pray too if I had a good life like any one of them.

After Ryker prays for our food and our day, the others fill their plates. When I don't take any food myself, Ryker serves me. Blake talks to Genevieve about the inn's renovations, and Isobel and Kieran divvy up duties for the day.

The conversations of these strangers give me a peek into this group's relationships. They're more than friends; they're a family. And it's nothing like mine.

A small ache settles in my stomach along with a wish for a sliver of what they have.

A wish for a home.

CHAPTER 5

· · · ● · ● · ● · ·

SHARONA

GENEVIEVE DRIVES DOWN THE dirt lane to Fable Farms. "I'm sorry I can't stay today."

My fingers brush against the pepper spray and pocketknife in my purse. "I'll be fine."

Today is the first day I'll be by myself at the farm. Yesterday, Genevieve stayed with me while I made hamburgers with Stephen. He threw out jokes and kept our conversation light.

He was so much like Saint.

For years, men ignored me or ordered me around. Anywhere from ignorant to abusive, I had a good handle on what to expect from men, and all my past experiences went into a box.

In two days, the guys at Fable Farms dented my expectations with their treatment of me. I shoved these new views into my overflowing box, but they didn't fit.

And it confuses me.

Genevieve parks in front of the main house. "I'll be back around one, but give me a call if you need me earlier."

"I will."

Unfortunately, I need my phone charged and powered on so I can contact her. But I endure the calls and texts I'm now receiving because Genevieve has been a lifesaver.

When my two nights were up, I was prepared for her to toss me out. But yesterday morning, she walked over from the little house in the back and worked at the inn as usual. All day, I dreaded her giving me a bill I couldn't afford. I finally asked her about it last night, and she told me I could stay until the repairs started next week.

Free of charge.

I had to lock myself in my room before I cried in front of her.

Genevieve drives away from the farm as I walk to the two-story main house. Cracks in the white paint on the exterior of the house indicate the years of wear. But like the inn, the house offers me a new type of comfort. What must it be like to live here with people who are not only friends but family? Who create lasting memories and share special moments?

The wood creaks under my foot as I step onto the porch.

Blake pushes the screen door open and holds it for me. "Hey, Sharona. I'll be helping out with lunch today."

Genevieve told me that Blake's her oldest brother. I found out she's fifteen years older than me, so Blake must be around my mom's age. He's handsome, but I find Ryker more attractive.

I shake my head as I enter the house. My mother lives like that. She falls for a pretty guy and lets her guard down. I can't be like her.

Blake leads me to the kitchen. He's laid out ingredients for sandwiches on the kitchen table they tend to use as an island. After I hang my purse with the aprons nearby, I stuff my phone into my pocket and wash my hands.

Blake rubs the back of his neck. "We haven't hit Willoughby's for groceries yet, so we're having sandwiches. I hope you don't mind."

"Food is food."

"I agree. We have stuff for about any kind of sandwich, so help yourself."

I grab the loaf of bread and give us both two pieces each. "Do you know what everyone eats?"

"I'm pretty much the only one who knows. Maybe Ryker, too."

"But the meals are for everyone. Y'all have to know what the others like in order to know what to make."

He shuffles to a drawer and grabs a few knives. "Not necessarily. Sure, you can pick a meal everyone will enjoy, but if you're trying to get particular—what kind of sandwich Ryker eats, what vegetables Stephen hates—I'm the man who knows."

"And what type of sandwich does Ryker eat?" I ask, curious about the guy who confuses me the most.

Blake slathers mayonnaise onto a piece of bread. "PB and J. Ryker's a basic guy. Either PB and J or ham and cheese. Nothing fancy."

I smile at the mention of peanut butter and jelly.

Rule Six: Peanut butter sandwiches are my friend.

Saint gave me the rules on my list to give me a life and protect me, but this silly one sneaked in.

My smile falls as I grab the peanut butter to work on Ryker's sandwich. Sometimes the two years feel like a lifetime has passed, and others, it's as if Saint was with me yesterday.

My phone vibrates in my pocket, severing my thoughts, but I ignore it.

Blake grabs a tomato and cuts it into slices. "I'm not too picky either. I think it comes with being a dad. Have to eat whatever the kids do."

"You're a dad?"

"Got two boys. Harding's thirteen, and Amos is eight. They come around when they're not in school. You'll meet them soon. We live in a house on the back of the property."

My phone vibrates again, so I pull it out. *Mom* displays on the screen.

"Do you need to take it?" Blake dips his head toward my phone.

I shove it back in my pocket. "No. It's not important."

My mom is a decent mother. At least, she used to be. But now, I doubt she'd ever worry about me. Her children aren't as high a priority as getting her next fix or another glass of whiskey.

Saint shielded me from the worst of her actions, but the three of us were happy once. We *were*. We made it work. Before everything fell apart.

I pull out a package of cream cheese from the fridge. Once I grab a bowl from the shelf and the sugar, I return to the table. I add half a spoonful of sugar to some cream cheese and peanut butter and whip it until it's blended.

"Whatcha doing?"

My spoon stops in the middle of a beat. "I'm sorry. I'm used to peanut butter with... never mind. I'll toss it out."

When I step away from the table, Blake holds his arm out to stop me.

"Wait, tell me what you were doing."

I drag the spoon through my concoction. "I was mixing peanut butter and cream cheese. It's a little treat my—I sometimes make." The memory of Saint and me creating our special sandwich flits through my mind. The Smooth Sandy, how Saint called it.

Blake smiles. "Sounds like a cheesecake. I'd be willing to try that."

"Really?"

"Sure. Ryker would probably like it, too."

Doesn't matter to me. But I make two Smooth Sandys for him and Ryker. Because Blake insists. Not because I'm trying to win Ryker over.

We bring the sandwiches to the dining room along with bags of chips and a few glasses of water. Blake walks out of the kitchen and rings the metal triangle.

When the others arrive a few minutes later, Blake points out the different sandwiches. They all take the one made for them, and I wait to the side of the dining room. Fortunately, I snag the chair between Ryker and Stephen. I glance at Kieran across the table. He's kept his distance since his outburst a few days ago, but he still puts me on edge.

They pray for the meal, and I stare at them. I'm not trying to be disrespectful—they have great lives, so the praying must be helpful. But with all their heads bowed and eyes closed, the prayer unites them. They set this time aside and come together, blocking out the world. It's like the balance in their busy schedules. A chance to take a breath, to rest from life's demands.

Blake wraps up the prayer, and they all dig into the food. Ryker tosses a chip into his mouth. My eyes flash to his sandwich.

What if he hates it? I should have asked first. If I keep messing up, they'll want me to leave. I might not trust them yet, but I don't want to be on my own this soon.

I look at Blake who stares at his Smooth Sandy with furrowed brows. He swallows the food in his mouth and meets my gaze. He gives me a wink.

Normally, I'd freak out. In my past, a man winking at me meant unwanted advances.

But of the Fable Farms crew, Blake's the father figure. Over these past few days, I've observed how he encourages them and guides them like a father does his children.

So his wink settles my nerves as the support he readily gives the others flows to me.

I pick up my sandwich which is loaded with veggies. Fruit and vegetables were a treat at our house since we bought cheap food with a long shelf-life.

But I wait to indulge myself as Ryker takes a bite of his sandwich. And frowns.

"I'm sorry," I say before he can get mad. "Your sandwich is different. It's peanut butter and cream cheese which is something I do every once in a while, but it doesn't have jelly. It's too overpowering. If you want—"

"Sharona, it's fine." He looks at the sandwich in his hands. "It's more than fine. It's really good."

"You won't hurt my feelings if you don't like it."

He smiles. "I'm being honest. It might be my new favorite sandwich."

Warmth rises in my cheeks. "I'm glad you like it."

He returns to his Smooth Sandy, and I sneak peeks at him as he devours his sandwich. Not counting Blake, it's been years since someone encouraged me or even offered kind words.

But Ryker likes what I made for him. And it's a huge compliment I never knew I wanted.

CHAPTER 6

· · · · · ● · ● · · ·

RYKER

AFTER WE GO TO church with the family, Kieran and I drive to our parents' house. My mom doles out a healthy guilt trip if we miss Sunday lunch.

Kieran steps into the house. "I'm starving."

I shut the front door and kick off my boots. "Mom said she invited Allegra and Kip, but they had plans, so it's just us."

We walk to the kitchen where my stepdad Cillian is stirring something in a pot on the stove.

Kieran crosses his arms. "If you're cooking, then I'm backing out."

Cillian spins around with the spoon held high. "I'll have you know I cooked for you your whole life, and you survived. Even loved what I made."

"It's nowhere close to what Gwen cooks."

"No arguments here. And for the record, I was only stirring the dumplings."

He gives each of us a hug as Tinka struts in, holding the hand of my four-year-old brother Brendan. He yanks free and takes his spot at the "big people's table." I give my little sister a hug, and my mom waddles into the room with my brother Ewan propped on her hip.

Cillian groans and removes the two-year-old from her arms. "Gwennie, I told you I don't like you carrying Ewan when you're so close to your due date."

She runs a hand over her round stomach. "And I told you to stop worrying."

He pulls her in by her waist and whispers in her ear. Kieran shakes his head, and I look away from our parents.

Tinka plasters her hands over her ears and shuts her eyes. "Can you stop? I don't want to hear or see my parents kissing."

As she drops her hands, Cillian snorts and turns to her.

"I was just saying—"

"No!" She shakes her head, her curls flying around her face. "I don't want to know what you said. Gross."

Cillian chuckles and kisses my mom on her cheek. She shuffles over to give Kieran and me hugs.

She pats my cheek. "I'm glad you came to lunch."

"Wouldn't miss it, Mom."

Her smile widens like I knew it would. Years after our lives were forever changed, years after she gave up the title Aunt Gwen, and she still beams every time I call her Mom.

We all find our seats at the table, and after saying grace, we pass around the food.

Mom places a piece of a dumpling in front of Ewan. "How has the new girl been working out?"

"Fine." I jerk my head toward my stepbrother. "She's still not a fan of Kieran."

He scowls. "I only yelled at her the one time."

My mom gasps. "Kieran, you didn't."

"I apologized."

I stir some dumplings in my bowl. "It's hard to get a read on her, but she seems to be better now."

"I wonder what happened," Cillian says.

"Don't know. She's not saying anything. But Blake said he'd try to ask her now that she's more comfortable around us."

Mom mashes up some stewed prunes for Ewan. "I'm glad we talked Blake into moving into Stella's house. He really needed his own place, and it's helpful having him close by."

We spend the next few minutes eating with limited conversation. After we have a quick dessert of oatmeal cookies, Tinka asks to be excused.

Cillian clears his throat. "Actually, I have some news I wanted to tell everyone. On Friday, Nic told me he's quitting."

My shoulders stiffen. Nic Kane has been Cillian's assistant for years. We tolerate him and his sister Ivy, but their family's actions have severed any chance of salvaging the Kane reputation. Or of remedying the pain they've inflicted upon my family or Isobel's.

Tinka frowns. "Quitting? He's not going to work for you anymore?"

Cillian expels a breath. "No, he's... leaving town."

"What?" Tinka's shrill voice ricochets throughout the room.

Kieran scoffs. "Good. His family's caused enough trouble."

My mom sighs. "Kieran, you're not being fair."

"Don't care. Not after what his mom and sister have done."

"What does that mean?" Tinka asks.

Cillian and my mom share a look. We've kept certain details from Tinka, about the Kanes and how our parents really died, but we might have to tell her everything. And soon.

Tinka sniffles. "Did he say why?"

Mom's eyes soften. "He said he thought it would be best if he started fresh. New job, new town. He wants to do something with his life and move on from being an assistant." She glances at Cillian. "He said after what happened, he thought now would be the perfect time to leave."

"Good riddance," Kieran says. "We'll be better off without him anyway."

Tinka lurches to her feet and sprints from the room.

My mom frowns at Kieran. "Was that necessary?"

He throws his hand up. "I'm sick of y'all giving Nic the benefit of the doubt. Tinka should know what his family has done."

"But this isn't how to tell her."

"He's not worth her tears."

My mom stands. "She's twelve. You know how big of a crush she has, and she's hurting."

She leaves, and Ewan starts crying.

Cillian picks him up and scowls at Kieran. "I'm going to ignore the fact you had a tone with my wife since we have to focus on Tinka." He lifts his finger. "But don't do it again."

"You can't tell me that this isn't for the best," Kieran says. "After what happened with Ryker's parents and now Isobel—his family makes a mess wherever they go. It was only a matter of time until Nic did the same."

My stepdad runs his hand down his face. "We can't judge him on his family's actions. Y'all should head home. We need to do damage control."

Kieran jerks to his feet and storms out of the room. I ruffle Brendan's hair before following my friend to his truck. He slams the driver's side door, and I climb into the passenger side.

He shoots me a glare before he reverses out of the driveway. "Can you believe them? They're mad at me for stating facts."

I prop my elbow on the window. "If anyone understands what the Kanes can do, it's me. But Nic hasn't done anything Kane-like. Even Ivy has been okay."

"I've tried to look past what his family did, but I can't. We'd be better off without any of the Kanes. Dad should have fired him months ago."

I take his curt attitude in stride. We've faced new obstacles recently. Kieran's adapted the best way he knows how—by developing a rough exterior to block the hurt.

"I don't get it," he says.

"Do you have to? Just agree to disagree where Nic is concerned."

We pull up to the main house, and Kieran parks his truck next to mine.

He turns to me. "I'm sorry. I know the Kanes did more to you than anyone."

I tap my fist against the window ledge. "I've moved past it."

And I have. Not a day goes by that I don't think of my parents and all the turmoil my family went through. I held onto the pain and anger until I decided to step up and become the reliable man I am today. I'm right where I belong, surrounded by those I love and honoring my family's legacy. The past might have shaped my life, but it doesn't own it.

The next day, I stroll into Hog Heaven around four. The afternoon crowd reminds me of my high school years. When I used to hang out here after school with my friends. When life felt simpler.

My mom waves at me and rounds the counter. "I told you that you didn't have to come."

"I wanted to check on her. Thanks for calling to tell me about y'all's conversation."

She glances over her shoulder. "She's taking it hard. Talking to you might help."

"I'll give it a shot. Is it okay if I take her to Mom and Dad's house?"

"Of course. Just drop her off at the house when y'all are done. Cillian's already home with the boys."

She waddles away, and I walk to the counter. Tinka sits on a barstool with a basket of fries in front of her.

"Hey, Tink. How was school?"

She drags a fry through a glob of ketchup. "Fine."

"Anything exciting happen?"

"Not really."

The drama queen, the bossy blond, the talk-your-ear-off little girl has lost her spirit.

I drum my fingers on the counter. "Listen, can we talk? We can go to the farm."

"I'm eating."

"We can take it to go. I wanted to talk to you."

"I'll have to ask Mom."

"Already did. She said it was okay."

She shrugs. "Fine."

Tinka's quiet during the short drive to our family's property. I steer my truck to the plot of land our father inherited. The house he and our mom were building sits in the tall grass, waiting for someone to complete its progress.

I park and turn off the ignition. "Let's sit outside."

We climb out and walk to our parents' unfinished house. Tinka crawls onto the slab foundation, and I sit next to her.

The land around the house was cleared for the building, but a circle of brush surrounds what was supposed to be the yard. A breeze rustles the leaves hanging from the trees as nature changes with the beginnings of fall.

I clasp my hands in my lap. "I love this spot. Secluded, peaceful. Only a special few get to see this."

Tinka scoots further onto the foundation and crosses her ankles. "Yeah, it's cool."

Well, this is getting us nowhere. "Mom told me about your conversation."

Tinka looks off to the side. "I don't want to talk about it with you. I don't want to talk about it with anyone. Nobody understands."

"Maybe not everything, but nobody will understand what you're going through more than me."

"Mom told me about the Kanes and our parents. I know what Verena did, and I hate her for it, but..."

"You still have a crush on Nic."

Her nose scrunches. "I don't want to talk about this with you."

"You have to talk to someone. It's not good to keep it inside."

She bites her lip. "It's... hard. The Kanes have hurt a lot of people." She huffs. "But I can't help the way I feel about Dominic."

I cringe at her use of his full name. Ever since she learned his first name was Dominic, she's called him that. He has a nickname for her, too. Calls her Goldie Locks. And while no one in my family likes this dynamic, Nic has kept his interactions with Tinka appropriate.

"You're only twelve, Tink," I say. "You'll move on and have plenty more crushes."

She glances away. "I know I'm young, and nothing could ever happen, but it hurts. I've liked him for years."

"It might feel like it's the end of the world, but trust me, when you're older, you'll find someone who you really love."

A deep sigh leaves her. "I guess."

I smile at the return of her theatric personality. "You remind me of Dad every day. Rowdy, dramatic, always causing trouble."

She grins. Then it falls. "Was it hard for you? When you found out how they died?"

My throat constricts as memories flood my mind. Both good and bad. Sad and happy. All life-changing.

"Yeah. Mom was there for me, but it was hard."

Tears form in my sister's eyes. "I wish I remembered more about them."

I lean back on my hands. "Let me tell you a story."

And I do. I tell her multiple stories about our parents until her tears are gone and she's laughing with me.

Because I can't bring back our parents. But I can give Tinka something to hold onto.

Comfort in our shared past.

CHAPTER 7

· · · ● · ● ● · ·

SHARONA

ON THURSDAY, GENEVIEVE DROPS me off for the lunch shift at Fable Farms. As I climb the porch steps of the main house, my dwindling time at McKellar Inn looms over me.

The renovations begin tomorrow. Without a place to stay, I'll need to leave town.

Which means leaving Fable Farms.

My situation might have started out as temporary, but now I wish for more time in this town. The cute bed and breakfast, the Fable main house, even the people have brightened my outlook on life.

I open the front door of the main house. "Hello?"

"In the kitchen."

My brows furrow as I walk down the hall. That sounded like Ryker. Blake is supposed to be helping me today.

When I reach the kitchen, I find Ryker sitting in a chair by the center table.

He stands and runs his hand over his blond curls. "Change of plans. I'll be on the lunch shift with you."

"Is Blake okay?"

He nods and walks to the fridge. "Yeah. He and his wife are divorced, and when she wants to see the boys, he insists on being there. He had a scare a few years ago when she tried to run away with them."

"That's awful."

When I met the members of Fable Farms, I thought their lives were perfect. But I've learned they all have messy lives like me. And that connection draws me closer.

Ryker reaches into the fridge. "Anyway, he'll be gone for a few hours. I told him I'd help you with lunch." He holds up two plastic containers. "Leftovers."

I grab one and open it. A mysterious tangy scent mixed with onions wafts from the gray sauce in the container. "What is this?"

"Beef stroganoff. You ever had it?"

"No, but this smells delicious."

As he places a bag of noodles on the table, his arm brushes mine. I pause at the contact, prepared for old feelings of discomfort to crawl over me. But they stay hidden, and my worries about men slide to the back of my mind. If these past few days have taught me anything, it's that Ryker's a good guy.

He pours the noodles into a large glass bowl. "My mom made it for dinner last night. She cooked extra for us."

His mom made him food? I can't remember the last time my mother cooked a meal for me. If I needed food, I went to Saint.

My eyes sting as I look at the spread on the table, at the food made by a mother who cares for her son.

A mother who loves her child.

Ryker gestures to the container of sauce. "You want to heat that up?"

I shake off the coat of hurt and hang it up, ready to analyze it another time.

Once Ryker and I have lunch on the table, he texts the others. When I ask about ringing the dinner bell, he says Kieran's checking on the fields toward the back of the property, so he wouldn't hear.

The four of them talk as they eat, but I'm too focused on the food. This stroganoff beats all of the home-cooked meals Saint or I made. The sauce has a tangy flavor with a small kick, and it's balanced with the right amount of sweetness. I polish off my plate, eager for a second helping, but my stomach can't fit another bite.

As Kieran brings his plate to the sink, a loud *moo* erupts from outside. Sounding extremely close to the house.

Stephen frowns and peers out the window. "The cows are out." He rushes out of the room.

Isobel follows Kieran out the kitchen door, and I hurry with Ryker to the front of the house. The screen door knocks against the frame as he walks outside.

Stephen stands in the yard, yelling at the cows and trying to move them. Ryker joins him, and I step onto the porch. A few of the animals stroll around the side of the house before Isobel and Kieran reappear. They join Ryker and Stephen in rounding up the cows.

I laugh as I hop off the porch.

Ryker turns to me with a grin. "Bet you're not used to this."

I shake my head.

He reaches into his pocket and holds out his phone. "Can you do me a favor? Could you call Genevieve and Tex?"

Stunned by his trust in me, a beat passes before I take his phone. "What do I say?"

"Tell them the cows got out and we need help corralling them. They'll bring some people to help us."

After I call Genevieve and Tex and relay Ryker's message to them, I give him his phone.

Kieran pats a calf nearby. "Baby, come on. Follow me."

I chuckle as he takes a few steps and the calf follows him, along with a few of the cows.

Ryker nudges me with his elbow. "Kieran's the cow whisperer."

Isobel rides out of the barn on a horse and comes to a halt next to us. "I'll push from the back. Y'all get the sides."

Ryker takes my hand, and even though my muscles tense, I don't pull away.

He gives my hand a squeeze. "Wanna help?"

"Sure."

He leads me to the side and teaches me the call they use with the cows. He shuffles farther away, guiding the animals toward their pen.

My eyes jump from Ryker to the others to the cows. Another laugh bubbles out of me as I absorb the odd situation. Trials and tragedies have flooded my life, and I miss having opportunities to laugh.

Ryker shoos a cow. "Sharona, keep an eye on that steer."

"How am I supposed to know which one is a steer?"

He glances to the side. "Watch out!" He dashes in my direction.

I step back, looking to either side of me. "What? What's going on?"

Ryker reaches me and grabs my waist. He pulls me to the side as a cow ambles past us, rearing its head as if it was charging.

At me.

Kieran distracts what I assume is the steer, and my heart pounds beneath my fingertips.

Ryker's grip tightens on my hips. "You okay? Sorry about that. He's got a nasty temper."

He runs his hands over my arms. My skin pebbles under his calloused fingers.

Instead of recoiling, my restless body settles at his touch. "Yeah, I'm fine."

He protected me.

Without hesitation and as if I was worth saving.

For years, I gave up hope of finding a good man. It stinks that I've found one when I'll be gone by the end of the week.

Genevieve hums as we drive away from Fable Farms. "That was exciting, wasn't it?"

Images of the Fable Farms crew herding cattle flit through my mind. "It was definitely unique."

"I tell you cows have a mind of their own. Were you able to find a place for tomorrow night?"

My mood plummets like a hawk diving for its prey. Tomorrow marks the first day of the inn's renovations. And the return of my runaway status.

I chew on my lip. "Yes, I did."

"Where? I know every inch of this town, so I can let you know if it's a good deal."

I fidget with the strap of my purse. "I called someone. And they told me I could stay in their spare room."

Every word spirals me into a bigger mess. In the years since Saint's death, I've had to push people away. A girl has to protect herself. That includes distancing myself from one of the few people who welcomed me to town. Even if she deserves better.

Genevieve nods. "Are they picking you up at the inn?"

I mentally slap myself. She'll know I'm lying when nobody shows to pick me up.

We pass the town square, and inspiration flickers like the flame of a candle.

"We're meeting at the park in the square." My insides feel as sticky as glue, the milky sludge covering the genuine parts of me.

Genevieve smiles. "I'll drop you off. It's been a joy to have you at the inn. You've been great company."

Her gaze returns to the road as if she didn't admit she considered my stay at the inn a pleasure. As if she didn't throw more sparks onto the fire of guilt building in my chest.

She parks outside the bed and breakfast, and I scramble out of her car. The sludge spreading through me chokes the crisp afternoon air and shatters the sunlight around me.

"I'll be in my room." I rush inside without waiting for a response, craving solitude for the first time in ten days.

When I reach my room, I shut the door and lean back against it. My gaze falls on my brother's jacket draped over the desk chair. "What do I do, Saint?"

The arrangement with Genevieve and those at Fable Farms has helped me survive for a week and a half. Once I venture off on my own, my money will be gone in a second.

My brother was right. If I want to survive, I need money.

Rule Five: All I need in life is money.

Hotel rooms and food will cost more than I can afford. Not to mention the laundry I'll have to pay for when I leave behind the washing machine and dryer at the inn. After tomorrow, I'll be stuck with an armful of clothes and a limited stack of cash.

I push off the door and drop my purse onto the desk. Maybe fresh air or rocking in a chair on McKellar's front porch will provide me with an idea. If nothing else, I'll have a little quiet. A touch of peace before I'm thrown into chaos tomorrow.

Voices drift toward me as I make my way down the hall. Genevieve is talking with someone. A man. Is it Tex?

"I'm sorry, sir," she says, "but I can't give out information about my guests."

"But I'm her father. She's only nineteen, and her mother and I are worried about her."

My back hits the wall, and I press my lips together.

It's him.

Jimmy Garfield.

My mom's boyfriend.

"Regardless," Genevieve says, "I can't tell you if she is or isn't here. That's confidential."

Jimmy grunts. "Fine." A few seconds later the front door opens and shuts.

Genevieve didn't confirm or deny I was here, but Jimmy's bound to be suspicious. And he'll come back.

I dash to my room and throw my stuff back into my duffel. Better to be packed and prepared than caught off-guard. If Jimmy is searching for me, leaving Mustang Cross may be for the best.

With my mind made up, I walk out to the receptionist desk.

Genevieve frowns at me. "Hey, a guy stopped by looking for you. He said he was your dad."

"I don't have a dad." Though I keep the whole truth from her, I give her this one nugget. I won't pretend Jimmy is anything other than a creep.

"Well, I didn't tell him anything," she says. "Do I need to call someone?"

I haven't had anyone on my side since Saint.

I have nobody.

"No," I say. "The person I'm staying with will meet me at the park tomorrow, and they'll help me."

An idea blooms in my mind. Not as beautiful as flowers, but it's the roots of a good idea. One night in a well-lit park is better than returning to the house I fled a couple days ago.

Genevieve's brow remains puckered. "You'll let me know if you need anything, right?"

I give her a smile with all the confidence of a girl with no worries in life. "Sure."

And the lies keep coming.

CHAPTER 8

· · · ● ● · ● ● · · ·

RYKER

KIERAN SLAPS THE DASHBOARD. "Are you even listening to me?"

I glance at him in the driver's seat. "Sorry, I was thinking about something."

Or rather some*one*.

Sharona's behavior from earlier bothers me. It was like her first day with us almost two weeks ago. She jumped at the smallest things and clammed up when we asked her where she was staying tonight. Even with me. I'm used to her keeping others at a distance, but she's grown comfortable around me. She lets me in.

And I didn't realize how much I liked it until today.

Kieran's truck reaches the intersection of Sunshine Road and Main Street. I set my thoughts of Sharona to the side and turn my attention out the window. Most of the stores in town are closed by this time of night, the activity on the street minimal. When I look at the park in the square, I notice a person lying on the bench under one of the lampposts.

I point toward the park. "Who's that?"

Kieran shrugs and drives past the square. "Maybe it's a homeless person."

"I don't know the last time I saw a homeless person in Mustang Cross. Someone would've seen them before now, and news would've spread."

"They could have just showed up today."

We reach Willoughby's Grocer, and he parks the truck. I head inside the store, grateful for the lighter crowd on a Friday night. After I buy a bunch of bananas and Isobel's almond milk, I return to the truck. When we're back on the road, my eyes once again drift to the park. The person is sitting up, and with the limited lighting, I can tell who the mystery figure is.

Sharona.

I unbuckle my seatbelt. "It's Sharona. Pull over."

Kieran follows my directions and parks the truck on the road's shoulder. "I thought she found another place to stay."

"Obviously not."

We stare at her from our spot inside the truck. She situates her large jacket around her, plumps up the duffel by her side, and leans back down as if she's trying to sleep.

On a bench in the park.

I sigh and run a hand down my face. How can I go to my house and leave her here, sleeping outside by herself?

Kieran's eyes narrow on me. "You're going to ask her if she wants to bunk at the farmhouse, aren't you?"

"She's sleeping on a bench, Kieran. She has no food, and it's dark."

"We hardly know her."

"She's been cooking with us for almost two weeks."

"Cooking food is different than staying at our house. When we're asleep, we're vulnerable."

"She showed up at Diane's with bruises. Running from her home and not knowing where she'd end up. I don't think she's an evil mastermind."

"I don't trust her.

"And I can't leave her here."

He leans back in his seat. "Looks like I'll be sleeping on Isobel's floor."

"Come again?"

He twists his hands around the steering wheel. "If this girl causes any trouble, I want to make sure Isobel's fine. I don't want her hurt more than she already is. Especially after these past few months."

"I don't think Isobel's going to go for that."

"I'd like to see her try to fight me on it."

I open the passenger side door. "I'll be right back."

After climbing out of the truck, I head toward Sharona. The park is deserted aside from the little brunette on the bench.

When I'm a few feet from her, she jerks to a sitting position. The light overhead shines on her face, illuminating her wide eyes. The fact I'm walking in the darkness pops into my mind, and I hurry to stand closer to the light so she can see me.

She relaxes against the bench. "What are you doing here?"

"I could ask you the same thing. Are these your new digs?"

"It's just for the night."

"So you have a place for tomorrow night?"

"Yes."

Of course, she does. It's called Casa de la Park Bench. She's probably coming right back here tomorrow.

I pinch the bridge of my nose. "Look, it's late. Why don't you come back to the farmhouse with us?"

"Us?"

"Me and Kieran."

She presses her lips together. "I'm fine. Thanks though."

Either she's still hesitant about Kieran, or she's nervous about being alone with the two of us in the truck. If I could get someone here she's comfortable with, maybe I could convince her to stay at the farmhouse.

I pull out my phone and dial Genevieve's number.

"Hello?" she says.

"Hey, sorry to bother you on a Friday night, but I need a favor."

"I'm in the middle of something. Can I call you back?"

"This is kind of a time-sensitive issue."

"What do you want?"

"I'm at the park visiting with Sharona. Found her chilling on a bench."

Sharona glares at me. It's the first bit of backbone I've seen from her, and a smile spreads across my face.

"At this time of night?" Genevieve asks.

"Yep. We're enjoying the night air. Thought you might want to join us."

She pauses. "This is a weird conversation."

A deep voice mumbles from the other line, but all I can tell is that it's a man. Maybe Blake.

Genevieve relays what I said to the person. Sharona squirms on the bench as I listen to the bit of muffled back and forth on the other line.

"Oh!" Genevieve's voice comes louder through the phone. "I'll be right there."

I hang up and plop down on the bench next to Sharona.

Her brows scrunch together. "What are you doing?"

"I'm waiting with you. Genevieve will be here soon."

She lets out a short exhale and turns to face me. "I said I was fine."

"You don't really expect me to leave a woman sleeping on a park bench, do you?"

She shrinks away, burrowing into her jacket. "I don't know what to expect from anyone."

Her words needle their way into my chest. Every part of me wants to protect this girl from whatever is forcing her to run.

An image of our steer charging toward Sharona flashes in my mind.

I grew up with the old-fashioned values of the men in this town. Men protect women. When my mom adopted Tinka and me, I became the man of the house. I have no problem being a protector and a provider.

But the sight of Sharona in danger yesterday unlocked a part of me I've never felt before. Protecting her became more than a desire. It was a need.

As she sits on this park bench, burdened by her circumstances, that need roars inside of me once again.

A light gust of wind blows a strand of her brown hair across her face. My hand twitches as I fight the impulse to brush her hair back.

With every day that passes, my feelings for her change and grow. She captures my attention whenever I see her. Her beauty, her soft edges, her secrets, all of it tempts me closer. I tossed flirting aside because of her circumstances, but part of me wonders if I could risk turning on the charm. If she'd be receptive to me.

I shake those thoughts off. Sharona has her own baggage, and I don't have time for a relationship.

Shoes scrunch against the grass a few feet from us, and I look up at Genevieve.

She stops in front of our bench. "Hey, guys. What's up?"

My head tilts toward the woman next to me. "Sharona's trying to spend the night at the park."

Sharona's eyes narrow. "Traitor."

Her unexpected fire sends a shiver down my spine. I mentally add *has a feisty side* to her list of tempting traits.

I drape my arm across the bench behind her. "You either come to the farmhouse, or I'm sleeping out here with you."

"You... you can't do that."

"Watch me."

Genevieve clears her throat. "Sharona, maybe you should consider it. If Ryker doesn't mind, I don't see the problem with it."

"Not a problem at all," I say.

Sharona looks between Genevieve and me as she fidgets with the collar of her jacket.

Her body sags. "Fine."

"Great," Genevieve says. "Why don't you ride with me, and we'll meet Ryker at the farmhouse."

I slap my thighs. "Sounds like a plan."

As they gather Sharona's things, I make my way to Kieran's truck. When I settle back in the passenger seat, my friend has a glare on his face.

"You know I couldn't leave her here."

"We don't have another room," he says.

"She can stay on the couch for now, which is the best option until we clean out... the other bedroom we have."

Kieran stiffens. "We'll check with Isobel."

"Of course."

He throws the truck into drive. "Whatever."

As we head back to the house, my mind is on Sharona. My feelings for her might be growing, but I can keep them on a tight leash. I help people, and this situation is just like any other.

Nothing about Sharona needs to shake me.

CHAPTER 9

· · · · ● · ● · ● · ·

SHARONA

As I walk into the farmhouse with Ryker, Kieran, and Genevieve, my confidence from earlier fades.

I didn't want to spend the night outside, but I would survive it. The bench kept me off the ground, and the light from the lamppost would discourage critters. I could take care of myself.

But thoughts of waking up in the dark with a raccoon on top of me fueled my imagination. Those little hands and beady eyes filled my mind and chased sleep away.

Kieran walks down the hall as Genevieve and I follow Ryker to the living room. He places my duffel on the floor by the couch.

He insisted on carrying my stuff for me, and I was too stunned to argue with him. The men my mom brought around the house were far from gentlemen.

Ryker threads his fingers through his curls. "You can have the couch tonight, and then we'll figure out sleeping arrangements tomorrow."

"This is fine. Thanks." At least, I have my pepper spray and pocketknife if I need them.

But I actually trust Ryker and his friends. A little. As I helped with lunches these past ten days, I got to know everyone. Even

Kieran, though I'm still warming up to him. Everyone treats me with respect. Like an equal. Like a friend.

Genevieve pats my arm. "You'll be good here. And if you need anything, give me a call." She walks out the front door.

Kieran storms past Ryker and me with a blanket under his arm. "I'll be upstairs." He scowls at me as he heads up the stairs to Isobel's room.

So much for progress. Now the angry one hates me even more.

Ryker touches my elbow. "Kieran will come around. You don't have to worry about him."

His voice reminds me of honey, slow and smooth. Different than how I expect most men to speak to women. And it trickles over the worry coursing through my veins.

I fiddle with the zipper on Saint's jacket. "It's fine. I get it."

Ryker walks away, and I assume he's locking himself in his room. But he returns with a pillow and blanket.

He tosses them onto the couch. "It's not much, but I hope it'll do until we can figure out where to put you."

"Thank you." It's more than what I expected tonight.

He taps the wall next to him. "We'll talk in the morning. This is the light switch when you're ready to turn them off." He steps into the hall and turns to me. "Goodnight, Sharona."

Fresh tears threaten to form in my eyes. When was the last time a person told me to have a good night, let alone mean it?

I blink the tears away. "Goodnight."

He disappears down the hall. After a few seconds, a door closes.

A deep exhale puffs out of me as I collapse onto my makeshift bed in the living room. Photographs of the Fable Farms family and friends hang on the wall. A lump forms in my throat.

My mom hung one picture in our house—a picture of her, Saint, and me all smiling. When challenges came my way, I wished on that picture, to return to a better time. Wishing for past happiness to flood into the present. But life only got harder.

Since there's no door in the living room, I change into my pajamas in the bathroom. I shut the lights off on my way to the couch. I try to sleep, but the pictures on the wall keep me awake. Even though the room is dark, the smiles and the joy agitate my mind.

This house is a home. And while I don't want to intrude on someone else's home, I'm greedy for any part of belonging.

My body bolts upright on the couch. What is that awful sound?

The sleep from my eyes clouds my vision as I scan the living room. The sun peeking through the curtains gives me no answers, only better light to see nothing out of the ordinary. Did I dream it?

The noise jars me again until I figure out what it is. I blow out a breath and flop back onto the couch. Didn't know a rooster would be my alarm clock.

"Morning."

My body twists toward the voice, and I faceplant onto the floor. What a morning.

Ryker kneels next to me. "Are you okay?"

The blanket tangles around my legs as I push myself to my hands and knees. "I'm fine."

I kick the blanket off and get to my feet as Ryker stands with me.

"Sorry. I didn't mean to scare you." He grabs two mugs from the coffee table and extends one toward me. "Coffee?"

My blood is still pumping after these past few minutes, but I grab the mug anyway. "Thanks."

"Hope you slept well. The couch is actually pretty comfortable."

"I slept fine." A couch beats a park bench.

"Everyone should be here soon, and we can see if it's okay with them if you stay. But you'll have to be on the couch for awhile."

"I don't mind, and I can help around the house in any way I can. I can cook and clean and—"

"Easy," he says. "You've already been a big help. I'm sure the others won't have a problem with this."

I drag my finger around the rim of my mug. "I don't want to be a bother."

"You're not a bother. We'll—"

A feminine screech interrupts him followed by a thump on the ceiling. I look up as muffled voices, both male and female, drift from upstairs.

Ryker sighs and lifts his mug to his mouth. "I was hoping to be gone by the time she woke up." He takes a sip of his coffee, his movements calm and languid.

Fast footsteps descend the stairs. Isobel appears wearing rumpled pajamas, her short hair wild.

She hops the last step and shoots a glare at the man next to me. "*You.* You've got some explaining to do. Do you have any idea how terrifying it is to wake up and find a person sleeping on your bedroom floor?"

"You should have recognized me." Kieran saunters down the stairs, every bit as disheveled as Isobel. He runs a hand through his bright red hair and scowls at her. "And I can explain just as well as Ryker."

"You would think best friends wouldn't argue so much," Ryker says.

Isobel huffs. "You love reminding me of that when I'm annoyed to no end."

The front screen door slams shut, and I jump. Blake strolls in with two younger boys. I place my mug on the coffee table, deciding I'll brave the caffeine when my body is calmer.

Blake frowns. "What's going on?"

Ryker jerks his head toward the opposite side of the living room. "We were just about to have a family meeting in the kitchen. Sharona, why don't you finish your coffee?"

I sit down on the couch but leave my mug on the coffee table.

Blake walks over with the two boys. "Sharona, these are my sons, Harding and Amos." He gestures to the taller one first and parks his hand on the second one.

They tell me hi, and the shorter one gives me a wave.

Blake pats both of their shoulders. "Why don't y'all stay here and keep Sharona company?"

The boys plop onto the couch, casual, as if we do this every day. And their proximity doesn't bother me. Even small progress is progress.

The others shuffle out of the living room to decide my fate. Last night I thought my bed would be a park bench, so people talking about me is the least of my worries. I just hope they let me stay.

The younger boy, Amos, faces me. "You living here now?"

"I don't know yet. Hopefully."

He points behind me. "My room was back there when we lived here. Now we share one since our house is small."

"Sharing a room with your brother must be fun."

"He touches all my stuff," Harding says, staring at his phone.

Amos scowls at him. "Because you don't share."

"My brother shared almost everything with me," I say.

"You have a brother?" Amos asks. "Did you have to share a room with him, too?"

Ignoring his first question, I keep the conversation light. "I shared a room with him when I was young, until I was about five years old."

Harding snorts. "Lucky. I'm thirteen. I should have my own room."

I press my lips together to avoid adding fuel to the teenage angst.

Amos shrugs. "Dad said when I get to middle school, we might get our own rooms."

Ryker enters the living room, and I stand, ready for the news. His friends file in behind him, the group as intimidating as a mob.

He gives me a smile. "We talked it over, and everyone agrees that you can stay."

A small breath ghosts out of me. "Thank you. I appreciate it."

"Not a problem. We'll let Stephen know as soon as he gets here."

"He won't be here until later," Isobel says.

Ryker frowns. "Why?"

"Esther's birthday is today."

"I thought that wasn't until next Saturday."

"No, it's today."

He rubs his forehead. "He's the worst at communicating."

Blake pulls his sons aside for a private conversation.

Ryker crosses his arms. "If he's not going to be here, we'll have to split his chores."

Isobel's gaze drops to her pajamas. "And I need to get dressed."

"We would already be dressed if you hadn't gone ballistic this morning," Kieran says.

"You mean, if you hadn't frightened me by slumbering on my floor without informing me."

Kieran flicks his hand like she's a pest and disappears down the hall. Isobel takes the stairs, and Ryker circles the couch.

He stops in front of me. "Let me know if you need anything, okay?"

Blake saunters toward the front door, but his sons return to the couch.

Ryker gestures to them. "Harding and Amos will keep you company in case you have any questions or need help. Just until the rest of us get back at lunch." He smiles. "Welcome to the farm."

He leaves, and I look at the two boys now arguing over the TV remote.

Babysitters. Two boys, much younger than me, are my babysitters.

But I don't complain.

My circumstances could be much worse.

CHAPTER 10

· · · · ● · ● · ● · · ·

SHARONA

A SMALL BIRD HOPS on the porch railing of the main house as I sit outside the next morning. The rockers at McKellar's are more comfortable than the chairs here, but the view of Fable Farms can't be beat.

Ryker clomps out of the house and onto the porch. "Are you sure you don't want to go to church with us?"

"No, I'm..."

My mind hits the brakes.

All my thoughts stall at the sight of Ryker in his church clothes.

He's wearing nicer boots than I've seen him wear, a blue button-down shirt, and a pair of dark jeans. I'm used to his worn jeans and T-shirts, but this cleaned-up look totally works for him.

The time I spend with Ryker jumbles my thoughts about men. But I can't get involved with a man. Even one as physically and emotionally attractive as Ryker.

He fiddles with his phone before his eyes flash to me. "Sharona?"

I study the chickens that pass by to cover my staring. "I wouldn't have anything to wear. I'll be fine here."

"You can wear whatever you have. Our church is lowkey."

Yeah, but is it full of people? "I'm good."

Kieran honks from his truck.

Ryker sighs. "I'll see you after, then."

He saunters down the steps of the porch, and my eyes wander back to him. One last look before he leaves.

After he climbs into Kieran's truck, they drive away and disappear down the lane.

Muddled images of early church days fill my mind. My mom said she went to church with my dad when she was pregnant with Saint. She came up with his name as she listened to Saint Peter and his service to the church. But by the time I was three, I'd only been to church a handful of times.

Then Dad left, and Mom stopped taking us. I saw no point in going back.

But church with Ryker might be nice.

With a huff, I stand and march down the porch. I need to stop thinking about Ryker. He wouldn't want my problems, and this situation is temporary.

Since I haven't had the chance to explore the farm until now, I take off toward the red barn. Some square hay bales sit inside, and two horses are eating in their stalls. When I walk to the cows, they stay away from me. I guess, too wary of the strange girl trying to feed them grass.

A little disappointed, I walk back and pass the henhouse. A flock of chickens wanders around the yard as if they can do whatever they want. One chases after me, and I run back into the house. And lock the door. Just in case chickens can somehow open doors.

I take a deep breath and plop onto the couch. I've had enough excitement for one day. Needing to decompress, I lie down and close my eyes.

When I startle awake, I'm not sure how much time has passed.

Ryker crouches in front of me with his hand on my shoulder. "Sorry to wake you, but I wanted to see if you were hungry."

He stands as I sit up and stretch.

"What time is it?"

"A little after noon," he says. "My mom's making lunch, if you want to eat with us."

"Lunch with your mom?"

"It'd actually be my whole family."

That's too serious. I just told myself staying in this town was temporary. Meeting more people, specifically Ryker's family, tangles me in more relationships.

More relationships I'll have to sever when I leave.

As I'm about to refuse going anywhere with him, my stomach growls.

He chuckles. "Sounds like you're coming with me." He holds out his hand. "Up and at 'em, beautiful."

My head spins. Beautiful? He thinks I'm beautiful?

While I'm reeling, I place my hand in his. He helps me to my feet, and we're inches away from each other. My mind protests how close we are, but my body won't budge.

Ryker frowns and squeezes my hand. "Sharona?"

"Oh, yes, right." I yank my hand out of his and scramble to my duffel. "Let me change real quick."

The drive from the farmhouse to his parents' takes less than five minutes. His parents' house spans a few acres, and their yard stretches from them to the neighboring house. Large windows and dark brown stone invite a more modern atmosphere to the rustic town.

Ryker opens the front door for me, and I step inside.

A little boy runs toward us, yelling like he's a warrior in a battle. Ryker circles around me. The boy reaches us, and Ryker picks him up and tickles him. The tender moment challenges what I thought I knew about men.

Ryker bounces the boy in his arms. "This is my little brother Brendan."

This is his brother? The boy must be around five years old. That's a big age gap.

"As you can see," Ryker says, "he's quite a handful. Bren, can you say hi to Sharona?"

The boy gives me a hearty wave. "Hi."

I smile. "Hi, Brendan."

Ryker looks around his legs. "And usually not far behind him is my other brother..." He jerks his head to the side. "Let's go to the dining room."

I follow him down the hall. Kieran is already sitting at the table. An older man with similar bright orange hair walks out of the kitchen. A pregnant blond woman settles another little boy into a highchair.

When she sees Ryker and me, she gasps.

She shuffles over with a smile. "Ryker, you didn't say you were bringing a friend."

He places his hand on my back, the touch steadying me. "Mom, this is Sharona."

She clutches me in a tight hug. "Oh, it's lovely to meet you!"

The unexpected act throws me off, and I stiffen.

She releases me but grips my arms. "I'm Ryker's mom, but please, call me Gwen."

I step back on instinct. "Nice to meet you."

The redheaded man offers his hand for me to shake. "Cillian Hennessy. I'm Ryker's stepdad."

Stepdad?

My brain whirls, trying to figure out more of the puzzle. First, the age difference between Ryker and his brother, now he has a stepdad? And his mother looks young. Definitely younger than her husband.

With every thought, I sink deeper into curiosity. Ryker's family has so many dynamics. Maybe he has a complicated life like mine.

Gwen rests her hand on her protruding stomach. "Ryker's told us all about you."

Ryker drags his hand down his face. "Mom, don't embarrass me."

Has he been talking about me? Like he thought I was worth mentioning?

Gwen walks back to the little boy at the table. "Tinka's at Marian's, so she won't be eating with us."

Cillian takes Brendan out of Ryker's arms and kisses the boy's chubby cheek.

Since I've been at Fable Farms, I've witnessed different sides of men. I've seen protective instincts with Ryker, charm and humor with Stephen, and fatherly actions from Blake.

But Cillian is so gentle with Brendan that I want to cry. He's a true dad. Which is something I lost years ago.

Ryker points at the younger boy with his mom. "And that's Ewan. You want to have a seat?"

I sit in the chair closest to me, and Ryker takes the seat between me and Kieran. Cillian walks over to Gwen's spot and pulls out her chair. She sits and turns to Ewan in his highchair while Cillian sits next to her.

Nobody acknowledges Cillian's chivalry toward his wife. So like a fairytale, and so similar to Ryker's manners. I didn't even know men still held out chairs, pushed them in, or opened doors for women.

Until I met the people of Mustang Cross.

Cillian says grace, and they all divvy up the food. Ryker serves me yet again, and my mind drowns under another new view on men.

Men learn about women and take care of them before they ask.

Gwen places a few cooked carrots on Ewan's small tray. "I talked to Shauna today."

"How's she doing?" Ryker asks.

"About as good as you expect. It's getting closer to the anniversary, you know."

He glances at me. "Shauna was married to Alessandro, our farmhand who passed almost a year ago. He was killed in a car accident."

"I'm so sorry," I say. "That must have been hard."

"It was. But we're getting by."

Cillian cuts into his meatloaf. "Tell us about yourself, Sharona."

I clench the fork in my hand.

Rule Nine: Family business is for family.

Saint told me all the time that nobody needed to know what happened at our house. Our business was our business.

Nobody knows our family like we do, he would say. *And nobody needs to know. Family business is for family.*

Ryker finishes chewing his food. "Sharona's a great cook."

My fingers loosen their grip on my fork, and he winks at me. Encouragement, like Blake's. Because I don't talk about myself.

He's protecting me yet again.

"Oh, that's wonderful," Gwen says. "You boys and Isobel need some good food. Can't eat sandwiches all day."

Kieran frowns. "What's wrong with sandwiches?" He points his fork at me. "Besides Sharona makes this peanut butter sandwich that Ryker loves."

My face must be as hot as concrete baking in the sun. Did Kieran just compliment me? And did he have to mention Ryker liking the Smooth Sandy in front of his parents?

Ryker scratches the back of his neck. "Yeah, she mixes peanut butter and cream cheese together. It's really good."

His mom's grin stretches wide. "That sounds delicious."

Fortunately, Brendan interrupts, and the conversation switches away from me. When we've finished our meal, Gwen stands to get dessert.

Cillian grabs her hand. "Gwennie, sit down. I'll get it."

"This is ridiculous," she says. "I can walk to my own kitchen."

"I want you to take care of yourself. And the baby." He stands and slides his arms around her waist. "Let me help you."

She sighs, but it's more a sound of relenting defeat than irritation.

Cillian kisses her jaw.

Kieran groans. "Stop, please."

Cillian scowls at him. "I'm not letting it get out of hand."

"This time," Kieran says.

Cillian dismisses him with a wave and walks to the kitchen.

Gwen chuckles and sits back down. "We're just kissing."

Ryker shakes his head. "I thought y'all would be on your best behavior since we have a guest." He leans toward me. "I apologize if they made you uncomfortable."

Just the opposite. Observing Cillian with Gwen has been like watching one of those safari documentaries. Saint and I used to watch them since we couldn't afford to go to the zoo. The people travel to the wild, immersed in the foreign elements. And the unknown—the new—fascinates them.

Over the past two weeks, Ryker has challenged a lot of my theories about men, but part of me wondered if he was an anomaly. A one-in-a-million type of guy.

But I've never seen a man treat a woman the way Ryker's stepdad treats his mom.

My mom's boyfriends were losers. Saint stuck by my side if a guy showed up at our house, and I followed rule three—never be alone with one of Mom's boyfriends.

Her relationships proved men weren't worth my time. I stayed away from them, but a few times, found myself without many options. Or landed myself in a situation I couldn't control.

Like on my birthday.

But my time with Ryker has changed my perspective. Would it be so bad if I hoped for a change, for a man who showed me how good a relationship can be?

For once, I think I'd want a man close to me, if it meant I got a little good out of it.

CHAPTER 11

· · · · ● · ● ● · · ·

RYKER

WHEN KIERAN AND I enter the house Tuesday night, my eyes lock on Sharona sitting on the couch. Blake, Harding, and Amos are in the living room too, along with Isobel, but I ignore them.

I walk around the arm of the couch and sit in the empty space next to Sharona. "How's it going?"

She blushes. "Fine. How was the recital?"

Tinka had a small dance recital during her class today, and the studio invited the families of the students to watch. Of course, my mom made me go. Unlike Kieran, I didn't complain because I want to support my sister. But an hour of preteen girls dancing the same routine strains even the most supportive.

I shrug. "About what you'd expect a recital to be. Lots of girls dancing around and flirting with Kieran."

My friend grunts as he reclines on the floor by Isobel's feet. "I couldn't get out of there fast enough."

Isobel chuckles and ruffles his hair.

The front door opens, and Stephen walks in, holding Boaz.

He sets the two-year-old on the floor. "I thought y'all would still be at Tinka's dance recital."

"We just got back," I say.

Boaz wanders toward our group and leans against Isobel's knees.

Stephen jerks his thumb over his shoulder. "I left my hat at the trough when I was watering the cows. Could y'all watch Boaz for a sec?"

I frown. "You didn't have to come out here this late. It could have waited until morning."

"It won't take long."

He walks out the door, and the others return to watching whatever's on the TV.

Sharona stares after Stephen, and a fire sparks in my chest. Based on her behavior toward men, I assumed she wouldn't be interested in any guy.

But if she was, I'd want it to be me.

Her attention snaps to me. "Can I ask you something?"

"Sure."

"I don't want to pry, but I've been wondering this for a while." She leans closer. "Is Stephen married?"

Though the fire inside me rages hotter, I smile at her whispering. "No."

"I haven't seen him with anyone. Did something happen to his wife?"

"He's never been married. Boaz is actually his nephew. He adopted him."

Her brows furrow.

"Stephen's sister Mary died a few years ago in childbirth."

She gasps. "Oh, I'm sorry. I shouldn't have asked."

"Don't worry about it. Stephen's doing well." And since I can't stand the unknown, I inflict more pain on myself. "But I don't know if he's looking to date."

She presses her lips together. "Okay."

"You know, if you were thinking... if you were interested in him."

Her eyes widen, and she lets out a sharp laugh. She clears her throat, trying to compose herself. "Sorry, you just surprised me. I'm not interested in Stephen. I was just curious."

Her words extinguish the fire inside me. "Oh. Okay."

She tilts her head and looks ready to ask me something—like why do I care if she's interested in another guy—but Boaz shuffles over and pats her legs.

She tousles his black curls. "Hey, there."

He hikes his leg up and tries to climb onto the couch. Sharona lifts him and situates him in her lap. He leans back against her chest like he doesn't have a care in the world.

Sharona lays her cheek on top of the boy's head. The beautiful runaway is as comfortable with Boaz as if he were her own.

Natural mothering instincts.

My mom said she developed those early on. She had to, with the circumstances dealt to her.

And though she's young, it looks like Sharona might have a few of those instincts too. She'd put her whole heart, devote her whole life, into giving her own child the life he or she deserved.

The front door opens, disturbing my daydreams of Sharona.

Stephen grunts, and I turn around. He holds his arm close to his body, his face contorted in pain.

I push off the couch and stride toward him. "What's wrong? What happened?"

Someone mutes the TV, and the others congregate around us.

Stephen winces. "I fell. Stupid gopher holes."

Isobel props her hands on her hips. "Is this another prank, Santos?"

"No, *Isobel*, it isn't."

Blake rotates Stephen's arm to inspect it. "It doesn't look broken. Does it hurt when I move it?"

Stephen mumbles in Spanish and scowls at him. "Yes, why did you think I was trying to keep it still?"

Boaz squirms in Sharona's arms, stretching toward his dad. She steps to Stephen's side, so Boaz is closer to him.

Stephen leans over and kisses the top of his son's head. "I'm okay, bud."

"He might have fractured it," Blake says. "We should get him to the hospital."

Stephen shakes his head. "I didn't get my hat yet."

Blake huffs. "Going to the hospital is more important than a hat. We'll get it later."

Boaz reaches for Stephen. "Daddy."

Sharona bounces Boaz and pats his back to soothe him. When her gaze meets mine, I give her a nod to let her know she's doing great.

I turn to Stephen. "I'll call your parents and let them know what happened."

Blake slips on his boots. "And I'll drive him to the hospital."

Harding steps to his dad's side. "Can we go?"

"No," Blake says, "y'all have school in the morning."

"We can skip it."

Stephen snorts though his brows remain scrunched. "Nice try, kid."

"I'll watch Harding and Amos," I say to Blake. "I'll stay at your house until you get back."

He takes Boaz from Sharona and ushers Stephen out of the house.

I face the others. "If Stephen's going to be out of commission, we're going to need reinforcements."

Kieran crosses his arms. "We were already stretched thin."

Isobel sniffles. "I can ask my dad if he'll let my brothers help. I'll ask Liv too."

Kieran scoffs. "Stephen's going to love that."

"He'll have to ignore his animosity for my cousin," she says. "This is my fault, so my family will pick up the slack."

I touch her arm. "What do you mean this is your fault? It was an accident."

Tears stream down her cheeks. "We wouldn't need all this help if Garrett hadn't left."

Kieran's face turns murderous. "Don't ever blame yourself for what that jerk did. It's not your fault."

"It is! I wasn't good enough for him, and now we're struggling."

"Isobel..."

She takes off running up the stairs.

Kieran scrubs his face with his hands. "I'll never forgive Garrett for what he did to her."

Sharona stands to the side, looking like she wants to run away from the conversation. But of course, she can't. We're technically in her room since we're using Isobel's old room for storage.

I clutch Kieran's shoulder. "Why don't you call Tex and ask about the boys helping out. Let me know what he says."

He drops his hands. "Yeah. I'll get on that." He stomps down the hall.

I turn to Harding and Amos. "Could y'all give me a minute and wait for me on the porch? I'll take y'all home in a few."

"Sure," Harding says.

He and Amos shuffle out of the house, and I'm left alone with Sharona.

"Sorry about that," I say.

She shakes her head. "I'm the one who's sorry. I wanted to give y'all privacy, but I didn't know where to go."

"Not your fault." I sit on the couch and pat the spot next to me. "Have a seat, and I'll explain."

She perches on the edge of the cushions. "You don't have to tell me anything."

"It's fine. The whole town knows, so it's not much of a secret. By the way, thanks for helping earlier with Boaz. You did great with him."

Her body slumps as if the tension has seeped out of her. "Thanks."

I lean back and rest my hands on my knees. "We recently lost someone, and it's been a struggle."

She nods. "Alessandro."

"No. I mean, yes, he passed. But we also had another friend. Garrett. He and Isobel dated throughout high school and got married two years ago."

"Oh. They were together a long time."

"Yeah, I think that's why it hit us so hard. But we knew his faults. The guys and I would catch his eyes wandering to other women, but he was careful around Isobel."

Sharona frowns. "I get that."

"A few months ago we found out he cheated on her. We don't know how many times. She finally asked for a divorce."

"That's terrible. I'm so sorry."

"Thanks. The room we'll eventually clean for you... it was Isobel and Garrett's. When they divorced, she didn't want to stay there anymore. We turned her room into an office and storage space, and we cleaned the upstairs for her. Just enough for a bed and dresser."

Sharona scoots closer to me. "She's been through a lot."

"She has." My thumb taps against my knee. "He cheated on her with a woman named Kizzy Kane. We aren't fans of the Kanes, but that's a story for another time. I just wanted you to know where Isobel was coming from."

Sharona reaches forward, hesitates, and lays her hand on mine. "Thank you. I appreciate you trusting me with this."

I flip my hand and lock it around hers. "Thank you too. For proving I *can* trust you."

She smiles, and the decision to keep my distance evaporates. I may not know much about her, but I plan to learn everything I can.

Because my heart says to give Sharona a chance.

CHAPTER 12

• • • • • • • • • •

RYKER

I CLOSE THE DOOR to Isobel's room and take the stairs as quietly as I can. When I enter the living room, Sharona stands from the couch.

Kieran appears, holding a mug. "Got Is some tea. She feeling any better?"

"A bit," I say. "She's worried about not helping today, but I told her we'd handle it, and I'd cover lunch."

Sharona nods. "I thought we would just make sandwiches today anyway. Something easy."

"That'll be fine since Blake took his boys for the day."

Many places in town, including the school, closed early today, so people could prepare for our fall festival this weekend. Blake had to pick up Harding and Amos, and he decided to take the afternoon off.

Stephen walks into the living room with his arm in a sling. "She still in bed?"

I prop myself against the back of the couch. "Yeah, she thinks she overdid it with the spaghetti last night."

"We need a chart or something," he says. "I can't keep track of everything she's allergic to."

Kieran stirs the spoon sticking out of the mug. "That's a good idea. I can't believe we haven't done it yet."

Isobel's developed food allergies over these past few years. Gluten, dairy, soy, pork, as well as any food high in histamine. We try to adjust our meals to accommodate her allergies, but we can't anticipate every reaction.

"I wonder if Allegra would help us," I say. "She's the food genius. Maybe she can give us some ideas for Isobel's diet."

"You want me to call her and see if she's available to talk?" Stephen asks.

I pull out my phone and dial Allegra's cell. "I'll do it right now."

Sharona steps around the couch and comes to my side. "Is there anything I can do?"

I shake my head, holding the phone to my ear. "No. We've been through this multiple times. She just has to ride it out."

The call connects. "Hello?"

My brows furrow at Kip's voice. "Hey, Kip. How're you doing?"

"Fine. You?"

It amazes me how little an English teacher can say. Aren't words his thing?

"I'm good, thanks," I say. "I was trying to get ahold of Allegra. Is she with you?"

Fumbling on the other end of the line reaches my ear.

"Hello? Ryker?" Allegra says.

"Hey, do you—"

"No, that doesn't go in there."

"Allegra?"

"Oh, sorry," she says with a laugh. "We're working on the desserts we're selling tomorrow."

"Are you at the diner?"

"Yes, what did you need?"

"Could I stop by? I wanted to talk to you about something."

"Sure, your mom's here, too."

"I'll be there in a few," I say before hanging up.

"You heading to the diner?" Kieran asks.

"Yeah." I walk to the door and slip on my boots. "I'll talk to Allegra and see if she has any suggestions about Isobel's allergies."

"You want me to go?" Stephen asks. "This is something I can do, if you want to stay here."

He's right. I can do more manual labor on the farm than he can with his fractured arm. He should go talk to Allegra.

But taking care of people is what I do.

I shake my head. "I got it covered."

"Can I come with you?" Sharona asks.

Kieran shoots me a hard look, but he'll have to get over his reservations. Sharona can help out if she wants. And I'll take any extra time with her.

She walks toward me. "I could go with you, learn about Isobel's diet, and maybe help with more meals. It'd give me something to do during the day."

Kieran frowns. "You don't have to do that." Meaning he doesn't trust her.

She fidgets with the long sleeve of her shirt. "I know I don't have to, but I want to help. If it's okay with you."

I give her a smile. "You're more than welcome to come with me."

She grabs her jacket from the couch, and I hold the front door open for her.

Stephen places his cowboy hat on his head. "Let me know if you need me. I'll keep working outside."

Sharona and I walk to my truck, and I reach the passenger side before she does. When I open the door, she hesitates before climbing in. I round the hood and plant myself in the driver's seat. As I start the truck, I glance at Sharona. She shifts in her seat, leaning away from me and toward the window. Her restlessness reminds me of a caged animal.

Realization hits me like a gust of wind. This has to be her first time riding with anyone besides Genevieve.

The first time she's been in a confined space with a man since she arrived to town.

I place my hand on the bench seat between us. "Hey."

Her gaze clashes with mine.

"You okay?"

She blinks then sinks into the passenger seat. "Yeah."

"You know you can trust me, right?"

"I'm starting to get that."

She's silent as I drive, and I let her have her space. A few minutes later, I park outside Hog Heaven. Only a handful of vehicles are in the parking lot, but I have a feeling we're about to meet a lot of people.

When I open the door to the diner for Sharona, she blushes. I follow her inside... and stop.

Perhaps I didn't think this through.

Every member of the Hershey clan is in the diner. Cousins, aunts, uncles, and in-laws bustle around as they stuff bags of desserts for tomorrow. A few of the tables are pushed together in the middle of the dining area to create a station for the makeshift assembly line. My mom and Cillian stand by Allegra, but Tinka and my brothers are missing.

Three less people to bombard Sharona.

Small blessings.

Sharona shrinks into herself, and I place a hand on her back. She jumps and turns her wide brown eyes to me.

"Sorry," I say, "I didn't think it would be this crowded."

And just as that word leaves my mouth, we snag everyone's attention.

CHAPTER 13

· · · · ● · ● · ● · · ·

SHARONA

Everyone is staring.

Kids, adults, young and old. All of them... staring.

Half of them continue filling bags of desserts while the rest swarm Ryker and me.

A brunette woman reaches us first and shakes my hand. "It's good to see you again. Sharona, right?"

My mind scrambles for recognition until I connect the dots. This is the woman from my first night in town.

The man missing one of his lower forearms steps to her side. He gives me a nod as he winds his arm around the woman's waist.

"Yes, hi," I say.

She chuckles. "I'm Allegra. You probably don't remember since so much was going on." Her gaze swings to the man next to her, and she slides her hand up his chest. "And this is my husband, Kip."

A deep groan erupts from a different man who nudges her side. "Ally, we're in public."

She throws him a glare.

He extends his hand. "Grady. We met when you showed up at the diner."

I shake his hand as another woman appears next to him.

She smiles. "I'm Beth."

"Nice to meet you."

Ryker wraps his arm around me, and I lean into him. For so long, I couldn't stand a man's touch. But with Ryker, I bear it.

With him, I crave it.

The four of them disperse only to be replaced by Gwen and Cillian.

She laughs and drops her hand to her baby bump. "Sorry, we're probably overwhelming you. How are you, Sharona?"

Ryker's hand slides up my back, distracting me from her question. I force myself to focus on his mother right in front of me.

"I'm good, thanks."

Her gaze shifts to Ryker. "Allegra said you had a question for her."

"Isobel had another allergic reaction," he says. "I wanted advice on meal planning."

"I'm sure she'd love to help. We're just filling a few more bags. Come on."

She and Cillian return to the group.

Ryker leans toward me, and his mouth brushes against my ear. "Everybody's getting ready for our annual fall festival this weekend. You'll love it."

A shiver rushes over me, but I push the confusing sensation away.

His hand drops to my outer hip. "Hey, you okay?"

Is it hot in here? I should have worn short sleeves. "It's just a lot of people."

He squeezes my waist. "Don't worry. I'm right here."

His words fill an empty space in my heart. If I've learned anything these past few weeks, it's Ryker is there when people need him.

He's a guarantee.

One I cling to in this moment.

He jerks his head toward the center tables. "Let's go talk to Allegra."

We walk to the people stuffing bags of desserts. Ryker leads me to a space opposite Allegra as she twists a tie around a cellophane bag.

She lifts her head with a smirk. "Can I interest you in breakfast?"

Everyone grumbles except for the man at her side, her husband Kip. His lips twitch, and his gaze rakes over her as if he's a painter seeing a masterpiece for the first time.

Ryker heaves a sigh. "No, thanks. We're fine."

"Sharona, do you want breakfast?"

"No," he says, "she's good too."

Allegra pouts, but a little girl hands her a bag and diverts her attention.

Ryker ducks his head toward me. "Ignore her. She tries to trick people with that a lot. There's an item on the menu called The Breakfast, but it's just a pile of sweets." He shrugs. "It keeps her entertained. She has a massive sweet tooth."

Allegra's head snaps in our direction. "Not true. I have a *food* tooth."

Ryker snorts as she walks around to our side.

She props her hip on the table. "What can I help you with?"

"I was wondering if you could give us some help," he says. "Isobel's still having allergic reactions. We need other options, and you're the pro at cooking."

The man with brown hair—Grady—frowns at Ryker. "I'll try not to take offense to that."

Allegra chuckles. "Let's go have a seat."

She leads us to a booth, and I flinch as Kip appears next to us. When Allegra scoots over on the bench, he sits next to her.

Ryker slides to the inside of the booth, leaving me the spot on the end. At least, I can escape for a little bit if I get too overwhelmed.

Allegra snuggles into her husband's side as he drapes his arm behind her.

She looks between Ryker and me. "So, you want food options for Isobel?"

Ryker discusses Isobel's allergies and her recent reactions. The more incidents he talks about, the more I want to help Isobel. The struggles she's gone through tug at my heart.

Allegra frowns. "I didn't know her allergies were this bad. I'm glad y'all are trying to be on the same page for her, but y'all can't remember everything."

Ryker folds his hands on top of the table. "Yeah, we were thinking of having a chart for us to refer to."

"That's perfect. Y'all could type up a chart of what she needs to watch out for and what she can have. And definitely read the labels of what y'all are buying. You might be surprised what they're made of."

"We'll read the labels more carefully, and one of us will get on making that chart."

In what time? They all work every day until the sun goes down.

Allegra leans into Kip's side. "I could research a bit. Maybe cook a few dishes, so we can test them out."

Her husband scowls at her. "Ally, don't overextend yourself."

"I want to help."

Ryker shakes his head. "No, Kip's right. Y'all are busy with work and have five kids of your own to worry about."

Five kids? What must that be like, to have a big family? To love someone as much as Kip and Allegra so obviously do?

The loss of what I don't have and maybe never will pelts me like a blizzard, freezing the small hope inside me.

But maybe I could have friendship. I don't know how long I'll be in Mustang Cross, but I can make friends, true friends. Ones that last a lifetime.

"I can help."

All eyes focus on me, but I don't back down. Friendships take compromise, and I can lower my walls to help a friend.

My hand wraps around the zipper on Saint's jacket. "I'm not doing anything during the day. I could research, type a chart, whatever you need."

Allegra's face brightens. "That would be wonderful. And whenever you're ready to try a meal, I can come help you. Do you know how to cook?"

Ryker snorts. "Oh, yeah. She can cook."

I clench my hands into fists to keep myself from touching my overheated cheeks. When Allegra and Kip share a look, my face burns hotter.

Ryker frowns at me. "Are you sure about this? I feel bad pawning it off on you."

"I'm offering. I'll go crazy with nothing to do."

Allegra giggles. "I get that. And you would be helping so much."

Grady walks over and slaps his hands on the table. "Now what was this about Ally being the cooking extraordinaire?"

"Who just spent hours baking desserts for tomorrow?" she asks.

"Only because you kicked me out of the kitchen, and Dad didn't side with me." He swings a glare to Kip. "And my best friend distracted me with my awesome nephews."

The corners of Kip's mouth curl up. "I was being a good husband. She promised me—"

Grady grunts. "Stop. She's my sister. I don't want to know what she promised you."

My eyebrows rise. Grady and Allegra are siblings. That explains their banter.

They continue bickering, and I pull in this moment for comfort. Memories of movie nights with Saint or eating midnight snacks when our mom finally went to bed shuffle through my mind like a deck of cards.

Kip lifts his hand. "Can we put this on hold? We need to finish up and get home. We've got a busy weekend."

Grady pushes off the table. "Always the peacekeeper."

He walks away, and Kip slides out from the booth.

Allegra bounces to the edge of the bench. "We'll see y'all at the festival tomorrow, right?"

"Sure will," Ryker says. "All hands on deck."

When Allegra stands, she rises on her tiptoes and wraps her arms around Kip's neck. She kisses him, and he pulls her closer.

My mouth drops open.

The PDA doesn't shock me. I've witnessed a few graphic interactions I wish I could erase from my mind. But what amazes me is the evidence of Kip and Allegra's love.

Whenever my mom and one of her boyfriends would kiss each other, I felt like I would vomit. They only seemed to be focused on the physical part of a relationship.

But Kip and Allegra look so in love that they can't help but show affection. Their love shines from a deeper connection.

Grady catches them from his spot near the bag-stuffing station. "Ally. Stop that."

She pulls back on a laugh and whispers to Kip. He winks at her and pecks her on the cheek.

Ryker clears his throat and dips his head toward the couple walking away from us. "Sorry. As you've probably noticed, many of the people in this town are overly affectionate."

I exit the booth and get to my feet. "It's sweet. It seems so freeing, so pure. The kind of love they have." I gesture toward him. "Even your parents."

He gives me a smile as he stands. "I guess so." He lifts his hand and wiggles his index finger. "I think you'll find the women in this town have the men wrapped around their fingers."

For years, I assumed men only wanted women to control. I wasn't going to fall in love with a man only for me to lose my independence. Nobody was going to control my life.

But I've found men who break the perspective I've always held.

Good men who want to take care of others.

CHAPTER 14

• • • ● ● ● ● ● • •

SHARONA

WHEN GENEVIEVE PICKS ME up for the fall festival Friday evening, my body thrums with adrenaline. Saint and I never had the chance to go to festivals and carnivals. Today feels like a momentous occasion.

If only Saint were here to share it with me.

I follow Genevieve as she weaves through the packed bodies in the park. A pillar of smoke rises from one of the booths. The smell of barbecue hangs in the air. We pass another selling popcorn with a long line trailing from the front. The sound of kernels popping from inside a large black kettle overlaps with the conversations around us.

Genevieve leads me to a stand filled with crates of vegetables. A sign with the words *Fable Farms* painted on it hangs above the booth.

I place my hand on the wooden slat in front of me as I admire the squash, lettuce, and various herbs. The beets catch my eye, and I smile. Saint and I had a competition one time. He dared us both to eat a can of beets as fast as we could. He won, but we were both sick afterward.

Genevieve hugs Ryker's family, but the blond man behind the booth gains all my attention.

Ryker lifts a crate of glass jars, his muscles bulging under his short sleeve shirt. He's dressed in his typical worn jeans and scuffed boots, and he couldn't be cuter if he tried.

No. I am not my mother. A man won't become my obsession.

But I could enjoy the view, couldn't I?

Ryker places the crate on a side table. When he turns around, his eyes land on me. My breath hitches as a smile spreads across his face.

He walks my way. "I'm glad you made it. How're you doing?"

"Good. You?"

"I'm great. How long have you been here?"

I gesture to Genevieve who's talking with Ryker's mom and another lady. "Genevieve and I just got here. This is pretty crowded."

"Yeah, I guess it can be a bit much if you don't know anyone." He tilts his head to the side. "I can show you the booths and tell you a little about the town. You want to walk around with me?"

My heart kicks its pace up another notch, and I tell it to calm down. He probably feels obligated to show me around. "Sure."

His smile widens. Almost like he wants to spend time with me.

After he speaks with his mom, he steps back over and places his hand on my back. "Let's start this way."

He indicates the left row of booths and drops his hand. The loss of his touch disappoints me.

"Mustang Cross was founded almost a hundred and fifty years ago," he says. "All of the founding families still have descendants in town. The Englands, Bradfords, Willoughbys, Honeycutts, and the Fables."

"Fable? As in your last name?"

"Yes, we were one of the founding families. We've owned our land since the foundation of Mustang Cross, but we've only had Fable Farms up and running for about fifty years."

"And you've lived here your whole life?"

"Sure have. I love it. Wouldn't want to move."

"How long have you been working on the farm?"

"Seems like forever. It's been a part of my life since I can remember."

We reach a booth selling wooden crafts, and Ryker gestures toward it. "The Honeycutts own the hardware store in town."

The people behind the booth are busy with customers, but I recognize Tex.

I point at him. "He was at the inn when I arrived."

"That's Tex, Isobel's dad. He was probably looking for Diane who's his sister. You'll learn a lot of people in this town are related."

When Ryker walks away, I hurry to follow him to another booth.

"Let's see... The Benedettis are another big family in Mustang Cross. They run Giuseppe's which is an Italian restaurant on Main Street. Really good food." He leans closer to me. "There's a rumor about the Benedettis. It only takes them one look to know who their soul mate is." He shrugs. "I don't know if it's true, but they do seem to fall in love young and fast."

Every new piece of information soaks into my mind. The town sounds so connected, so personal. Like a family.

Ryker rubs the back of his neck. "I'm talking too much."

"No, it's interesting."

"We're a close-knit community, but don't let it scare you."

We reach the next booth. Allegra stands behind a table overflowing with bags of desserts.

She waves at us. "Hi, guys! Do you want a bag of brownies? Cookies?"

Grady elbows her out of the way. "Or do you want to try my hot chocolate?"

Allegra shoves his arm and props her hands on her hips. "Grady, this isn't a competition."

"Says the woman who taunted me when Cillian took ten bags of sweets without ordering a single cup of hot cocoa." He turns to us. "Y'all want something?"

Ryker motions for me to order first.

But I can't afford to spend my money on sweets. I need to save it in case I lose the job at Fable Farms or they kick me out.

I shake my head. "I'm good."

Ryker takes out his wallet. "Go ahead and pick something. My treat."

So I can be indebted to him? No, thanks.

My head shakes faster as I try to turn him down. "Honestly, I'm fine."

He ducks his head to meet my gaze. "Please? I want to do this."

The weight of his stare traps me. My heart takes off again, trying to beat its way toward the cute guy against my better judgment.

"I guess I could have a hot chocolate," I say.

Grady grins. "Wise choice." He grabs a paper mug and fills it with hot chocolate from a dispenser.

Allegra groans. "Sharona, you were supposed to choose something from me!"

Ryker snorts and hands her some cash. "I'll take a bag of whatever you got. Happy?"

She lunges for a bag next to her. "Super."

Grady scoffs and holds the cup out to me. "She's nothing but a bully. You'll scare customers away, Ally."

She hands Ryker a bag of sweets as she bickers with Grady. Ryker and I make our escape, and I hold the warm cup between my hands. Steam wafts toward me, and the sweet aroma of cocoa hits my nose.

Ryker opens his bag and sticks his hand inside. "You want one? Allegra bakes the best brownies."

I lift my cup. "I got a hot chocolate."

"Sharona, I'm obviously not going to eat all these by myself."

I bite back a smile. "I can have one later. I don't have a big sweet tooth."

He swallows the food in his mouth and gestures to me with the brownie in his hand. "What's your favorite food?"

I jerk my thumb behind us. "Actually, fruits and veggies. I didn't get them often growing up, so they were sort of a treat. Your booth's probably my favorite."

He smirks. "Good to know."

We approach a section of the festival set up away from the booths. People wander through a pumpkin patch to our left. To our right, a tractor pulls up with a trailer attached to the back of it. People sit on top of the hay bales lining the perimeter of the trailer.

A blond girl, maybe around middle school age, stops in front of Ryker. "I need to borrow five dollars."

He waves her away. "Go ask Kieran."

"He told me to ask you."

"Of course he did." He pulls out his wallet and thumbs through his cash.

The girl looks over her shoulder, her curls bouncing with the movement. "Come on."

Ryker holds up a five-dollar bill. "What's the magic word?"

She latches onto his arm. "Please, please, please."

He shakes her off and offers her the cash. "Okay, fine."

She snatches it from him. "Thanks, I'll pay you back." She spins around and weaves through the crowd, disappearing from sight.

He shoves his wallet into his back pocket. "Sorry about that. Siblings, right?"

Siblings? Is that his little sister? He's an older brother, just like Saint and me.

And that bond, the similarity between Ryker and me, only tugs me closer.

"I didn't know you had a sister."

Ryker closes the bag of treats. "That's Tinka. She wasn't at our family lunch."

"I have a brother." I flinch at my use of the present tense.

"Yeah? Older or younger?"

"Older."

He dips his head in the direction his sister ran off. "Tinka's a bit younger than me, but we're close. Until a few years ago, it was just the two of us." He laughs, short and loud. "It's a little complicated."

Complicated is my middle name.

"What do you mean?" I hold up my hand. "No, wait. You don't have to tell me." Even though I'm dying to know more, it's not right for me to ask. I've kept most of my life a secret from him.

"It's okay. I'm fine with telling you." He places his hand on my back and guides me off to the side. "My mom raised Tinka and me by herself for a long time. She only married Cillian, who's Kieran's dad, a few years ago. If you count the baby on the way and Kieran and his brother, I have five stepsiblings."

I hang on every word, longing for the complicated of someone else. Wanting to share with someone what we have in common. Wanting that connection.

Ryker jerks his head to the side. "Do you want to go on the hayride?"

He wants to spend more time with me? I mean, I want to spend more time with him, but I thought he was just fulfilling his obligation as my new landlord. You know, being hospitable to your tenants.

Before I can respond, Stephen joins us, his arm snug in its sling.

He tips his chin toward me. "Sharona." He scowls at Ryker. "I stopped by the farm and saw hogs rooting in the pasture."

Ryker frowns. "Again?"

"Yeah, there were about sixteen, but I had trouble shooting any of them."

Ryker throws his hand up. "If they keep messing up our fields, we're going to have a problem."

"It's already a problem." Stephen takes out his phone and hands it to Ryker. "I took pictures of the field."

Ryker's jaw clenches as he swipes his finger across the screen. He releases a groan and shoves the phone back at his friend. His eyes flash to me. In an instant, his tension smooths away.

He touches my arm, and I realize I'm prepared to flee, my body poised away from him.

"I'm fine," he says. "Just frustrated."

My body relaxes as if it was waiting for his reassurance.

Stephen pockets his phone. "I'm heading back to the farm. I could use your help since I'm handicapped."

Ryker nods. "Give me a sec, and I'll be right behind you."

Yet another friend he's helping. Ryker gives most of his time to his friends. I think he'd say yes to anyone and do almost anything for those he cares about.

As Stephen leaves, Ryker touches my arm again as if he's testing me, to see what I can handle. When I allow it, he pulls me away from the crowd.

"I'm sorry if I scared you," he says.

Just like before, his words flow a river of calm in my direction. Like finding the exit to a labyrinth after hitting multiple dead ends.

I shake my head. "I'm fine."

"I have to leave, but are you coming back tomorrow? I would offer to drive you myself, but I have a hectic schedule this weekend."

"I'm not sure. I'll ask Genevieve."

"Come back tomorrow, if you can, and I'll give you that hayride."

"Sure. Yeah, I'll try."

"I'll see you later."

When he walks away, I'm slammed by the effect he has on me. Because he saw my worries and wanted to take them away. He saw my fear and soothed it. I was ready to run, but he stopped me and convinced me to stay.

Because he saw me.

CHAPTER 15

· · · ● · ● · ● · ·

SHARONA

THE MOMENT WE ARRIVE at the festival the next evening, Genevieve takes off. I stand among the passing townsfolk, a girl without a home obstructing the connected lives around her.

Goosebumps erupt across my skin, and I rub my arms, trying to warm myself up. I should have brought Saint's jacket to ward off the early November breeze.

To give me armor against the attack of homesickness.

"Sharona!" Ryker emerges from the Fable Farms booth a few feet away with a smile. "You made it."

When he texted me this morning and asked if I would be coming to the festival, I spent a long time staring at his message. I wanted to see him, without a doubt. But I didn't want to place my hope in his hands only for him to crush it.

My fingers clench around my upper arm. "I did. Genevieve told me to check out more of the food booths, that some are giving away free samples."

"I haven't had a chance to walk around much," he says. "The day's flown by."

"Have y'all been busy?"

"Swamped. But it's good for business. And I know I promised you a hayride—"

My stomach sinks. He's going to cancel. Why didn't I stay at the farm? I knew better than to trust a man's promises.

"—but do you want a hot chocolate, first?"

Wait, what?

He places his hand on my arm. "Thought something warm would be good, and you liked Grady's hot chocolate yesterday, right?"

I nod, my words shriveled up in my dry mouth.

He frowns. "You're cold. Here." He shrugs out of his jacket and drapes it over my shoulders.

The action makes me so sick with want. Want of belonging. When I'm with Ryker, it's hard for me to remember my stance on men.

And that's dangerous. I'm not my mom who treats men like paychecks, only there to provide money, food, and shelter. I shouldn't enjoy taking hot cocoas and warm jackets from a man. Even if that man is Ryker.

I scramble out of his jacket. "No, I'm fine."

"Sharona, your skin was ice. Just take it."

I shake my head and hold the jacket away from me. "No, I can't."

Ryker's hands remain by his sides.

My fingers clench the rough fabric, and my muscles bunch in my shoulders. "Take it back."

He steps closer, leaving the jacket sandwiched between us. His hand envelops mine where it's still gripping the material. "Please, wear my jacket."

My reluctance melts away. As much as I don't want to take from a man, what if he willingly gives to me instead?

I step back and shove my arms into the bulky sleeves of his jacket. "Thanks."

His lips twitch. "Sure."

Heat bursts through my cheeks. "So... hot chocolate?"

He places his hand on my back. "This way."

We buy another hot chocolate from Grady and walk through the booths in the direction of the hayride. More people mingle through the park than yesterday. A few stop Ryker to talk to him, and he introduces me to all of them. I forget most of the names, but I like seeing Ryker in his element.

When it becomes thick with people, he guides me between two booths through a back way. Two people stand a few feet from us.

Genevieve and Tex.

She looks on the verge of tears. Tex hangs his head as she talks to him. Ryker's gaze lands on them, and he stops.

He gestures to the side. "Let's go back this way. That looks private."

Though I'm curious about their conversation, it's none of my business. I have my own secrets, so Genevieve can keep hers.

Ryker leads us to the hayride station as the tractor pulls up. The people who have returned from the hayride get off the trailer. Another group replaces them, and Ryker and I follow. When he asks me where I want to sit, I point to a spot toward the back, away from most of the people. He shuffles over and sits closest to the others, leaving me on the end. Giving me a chance to breathe.

He scoots closer to me, and I turn my face into his jacket to hide my smile.

And his scent slams into me. Musky, woodsy, and calming. It must be on his collar. Or on every inch of his thick jacket.

As we wait for everyone to get settled on the trailer, Ryker chats with an older couple across from us. He casually reaches for my hand and links our fingers together.

My reservations about him touching me disappear. Having him as my anchor steadies me in the turbulence of the world.

When the trailer is stuffed with people, the man driving the tractor pulls away.

Ryker ends his conversation and turns to me. "So what have you been up to today?"

"I was working on the chart for Isobel. I categorized some of the most common foods high and low in histamine, but I don't know if it's finished."

When he shrugs, his shoulder brushes against mine. "Can't put every food down. That'd be a long list."

We fall silent as the hayride continues. A few people have side conversations, and I search for a topic, greedy for more information about Ryker. His thumb brushes the back of my hand, and the sweet action gives me the confidence I need.

"Yesterday... you sounded like Fable Farms was important to you."

"It is," he says.

"It seems like a lot of family history." What must it be like to have so much history? A family he can trace through the years? He has a sense of certainty, of belonging. He came from somewhere.

I don't have that.

He nods, bringing my focus back to him. "Yeah, my mom's always instilled in me a love of the farm and my family."

"But she doesn't live close to you?"

"Not yet. She and Cillian are building a house on the property, but until it's finished, they're living in what used to be Cillian's house. They keep jumping from house to house as our family keeps growing."

"You like having a big family."

He smiles. "I do. It's prepared me for one of my own someday."

His steady gaze holds mine, and my heart thrashes in my chest. Like it wants to join this little family he wants to have one day.

As if I belong with him.

A man next to Ryker asks him a question, and he breaks away to answer him. I pluck at the hay bale beneath me and cool off from the intense moment.

The breeze picks up as the trailer trundles along. I want to keep holding Ryker's hand, but I also want to snuggle into his jacket. Warmth wins over his touch, and I release his hand and wrap my arms around myself.

He frowns. "Sorry about the cold."

"Not like you can control it."

He chuckles. "True. But I might be able to help warm you up."

My eyes widen as he wraps his arm around my waist. When he pulls me closer, I give in and nestle into his side. Fighting my attraction to him is exhausting.

He squeezes my hip. "Is this okay?"

"Yes." The word comes out breathy, and my cheeks burn. I'm so flustered around him.

Someone gets his attention, and I use the distraction to process my current situation.

I'm pressed into a man's side. His arm holds me tight. His thumb brushes up and down my hip.

And I wish I could stay on this hayride for hours.

All because of a man.

CHAPTER 16

• • • • • • • • • •

RYKER

AFTER I HELP SHARONA climb off the trailer, I thread our fingers together. She blushes and glances away but leaves her hand in mine.

It's taken me weeks to draw her closer, but every push and pull between us has been worth it. I know what it's like to touch her, take care of her, see the sides of herself she keeps from everyone else.

And I couldn't stop myself from pursuing her even if I tried.

We stay along the edge of the booths, and I point out a few of the other families in town.

I give Sharona's hand a squeeze. "So, you never did say. Where are you from?"

She balks. "Fort Worth."

"Wow, that's quite far. Did you move here by yourself?"

"I'm, uh, I just moved... to town."

Which doesn't answer my question and only shoots my pulse to the sky.

"We don't have to talk about it," I say.

She stiffens and tries to pull away from me, but I grip her hand tighter.

I move into her line of sight. "Sharona, it's okay. You don't have to tell me anything."

"It's not that I don't want to. I... don't come from a good situation. And you should know this stuff. If a random person was in my house, I would want to know everything about them."

"I do want to know everything about you, but I'm not going to force you to talk about it."

She presses her lips together as if she's holding her breath.

"Breathe, Sharona."

Her shoulders fall, and she exhales.

I take a chance and raise my free hand. When she doesn't flinch, I brush my knuckles along her jaw. "You can tell me when you're ready."

"Please don't hate me."

My knuckles skim down her neck. "I could never do that." My hand freezes. "But it's not illegal, right?"

"I did nothing illegal. I promise."

I step back but keep our hands entwined. "Then that's enough for me."

A few leaves fall around us as we walk to the pumpkin patch. The breeze grows stronger, and Sharona pulls my jacket tighter around her. The chill in the air sinks through my shirt, but the view of Sharona in my clothes is worth being a little cold.

I lead her away from the townsfolk in the park. "I love fall."

She shrugs. "It's not really my favorite."

"Why's that?"

"Nothing good happens in fall."

"You have Thanksgiving, cooler weather—"

She mumbles something so low I miss it.

"What did you say?"

"It's not important."

I tug on her hand, pulling her closer to me. "Will you please tell me?"

She sighs. "I said birthdays."

"Birthdays? They're not good in fall?"

"Not mine."

"Wait, when's your birthday?"

"Can we talk about something else?"

"No."

Her lips twitch. "My birthday is October thirty-first."

I do the math in my head and think through the past few weeks. "That was the night you came to town."

Instead of celebrating her birthday, she felt like she needed to run away.

As I take in her features, the first thoughts I had about her age hurtle into me.

Thoughts that she might be in high school.

My stomach twists, and I snatch my hand back. "I probably should have asked this before now, but you're at least eighteen, right?"

Her brows draw together before a grin spreads across her face.

And she laughs. She gives me another one of her intoxicating laughs, and it settles into my chest.

She waves her hands through the air. "Sorry. Your reaction is just... I'm not used to someone being worried I'm too young."

Warning bells.

Sirens.

Foghorns.

All the signals go off in my head.

My expression must not be what she wants because her laughter fades. "I'm nineteen."

The rock in my stomach rolls away. Young but legal. Good. I would have stayed away, but it would have been hard.

I grip the front of the jacket and tug her toward me. A small gasp puffs out of her, but she doesn't pull away. Even stumbles closer. When I raise my hands toward her face, I allow her to stop me. She swallows hard, but once again, lets me in.

She always lets me in.

I cradle her face between my palms and press my forehead to hers. "I hope your next birthday is better."

She shudders out a breath. "Doubtful."

"It will be. I'll make sure of it."

Kieran comes up to us, and Sharona shrinks away from him. I move her behind me, keeping my hand on her hip. I want her to know she can trust me to protect her. Even from my grumpy friend.

Kieran looks between us. "Sorry to interrupt. Gwen's water broke."

My eyes widen. "What? Where is she?"

"My dad's taking her to the car, so they can go to the hospital."

I grab Sharona's hand and pull her along with me as we weave through the congested aisles. "Do they need help with the booth?"

Kieran keeps pace with me. "I think your aunt said your grand-parents were stepping in."

We reach the Fable Farms booth, and my grandparents have joined my great-aunt and uncle. But my little brothers drift around the small space. Waiting to create havoc like boys do.

I turn to Kieran. "If my grandparents can take Brendan and Ewan, the rest of us can cover the booth."

"On it," he says before rounding the front table to talk to my folks.

I lead Sharona away for some privacy. As I stare down at the woman in front of me, old Abe Bradford's words float through my mind.

He once said, "A man rules the home, but a woman rules the man." He and his wife Myrtle had laughed, so I took it as a joke.

But his words stuck with me. I couldn't help but hear the truth in them. Men take care of their households and their families, but the right woman could bring a man to his knees.

And for Sharona, I'd willingly fall.

I rub my thumb over the back of her hand. "I have to stay and help."

"What else is new?"

I frown.

She shakes her head. "You're always helping other people. I think most of your time is actually spent doing things for others than for yourself."

I never notice how much time I devote to others. But Sharona obviously has. Is she watching me as much as I've been watching her?

I squeeze her hand. "I'll see you at the house."

"Sure."

"Keep my jacket. I'll get it from you tomorrow."

The corners of her mouth curl up as she nods.

We walk back to the booth as Genevieve shows up with red-rimmed eyes.

She blinks. "You ready?"

Sharona frowns. "Yes. Are you okay?"

Genevieve flicks her hand. "I'm just ready to go."

Sharona turns to me. "I'll see you later."

I lift our clasped hands and kiss the back of hers. "I'll see you later, beautiful."

She blushes, and I want to call her beautiful again and again.

Just for the sweet blush that tells me I affect her as much as she affects me.

CHAPTER 17

· · · ● · ● · ● · ·

SHARONA

BEFORE I COOK DINNER, I rest on the couch and relive my time with Ryker this weekend. New memories settle in my mind and replace old ones.

Ryker buying me hot chocolate. Him giving me his jacket. Him holding my hand. How he wrapped me in his arms on the hayride.

He was so sweet on me.

I haven't had the chance to talk to him or any of the group much today. After spending the weekend working the festival, they had chores to catch up on. But I'm aching for some more time with Ryker.

Me. Sharona Bennett. Wanting to be alone with a man. Never thought that would happen.

The front door of the main house opens. Someone marches down the hall and appears by the living room.

Ryker. With a scowl. Shirtless.

My eyes trail from his muscular arms to his flat stomach. He faces the wall and chucks the shirt onto the floor. He props his hands on his hips, and I drink in the tan muscles on full display.

I really need to say something. Let him know I'm here. But my mind is too busy admiring the hot man a few feet from me.

He spins around and meets my gaze. My cheeks feel as hot as they did the one time Saint dared me to eat a bowl of peppers.

A small smile plays on Ryker's lips. "You were there when we moved you into your room, right?"

While they helped with the festival this weekend, Ryker and his friends were in and out of the house at random times. Since I was staying in the living room, I got little sleep. Ryker apologized for the lack of privacy. He and Stephen spent today cleaning the spare room for me. They relocated the office and most of their storage upstairs.

I clap my hands over my eyes. "I was just sitting for a bit before I started dinner. I won't look."

"I'm a twenty-three-year-old guy. I don't mind a pretty girl checking me out."

My cheeks are on fire. "I'm not checking you out."

"That's a shame."

"Go put on a shirt."

He sighs. "If you insist. But know you're missing out."

Once he walks away, I cup my face and hope the heat I feel isn't noticeable on my cheeks. I've never had to worry about being attracted to a guy before. How do people keep from floundering under their attraction when they like a person?

When Ryker returns to the living room, he's wearing a white T-shirt. I'm equal parts relieved and disappointed to see all that muscle hidden away.

I grab the pillow next to me and wrap my arms around it. "Can I know why you felt the need to walk into the house shirtless?"

"Not my doing." He saunters over and sits next to me on the couch. "It's one of Stephen's pranks."

One of? Does Stephen prank people often?

I clutch the pillow tighter. "It's been so busy, I haven't had the chance to ask. How's your mom and the baby?"

"Both good." He takes out his phone and scrolls through it. He turns it around to show me a picture of a baby bundled in a pink blanket. "Maureen Hennessy."

"That's a beautiful name. How'd they pick it?"

"Cillian has Irish roots, and all the boys have names ending in *n*. Kieran, Donovan, Brendan, Ewan. My mom didn't mind keeping the tradition for Maureen."

"Well, I love it. It's feminine and unique."

He winks at me. "Like yours."

I squeeze the pillow in my lap. "Yours, too."

He chuckles. "My name's unique and feminine?"

I nudge him with the corner of the pillow. "I meant the unique part."

"I guess. My mom said Cillian's over the moon."

He drapes his arm across the back of the couch, and my body settles closer to his.

"He adopted Tinka after he married my mom," Ryker says, "but she says he's always wanted another daughter."

"Can I ask... there's a big jump between the new baby and you. Was your mom young when she had you?"

He runs his fingers through his hair. "Actually, my mom's not actually my mom. It's more of the *complicated* I was telling you about."

Which only intrigues me more. But it's unfair for me to keep asking.

I scoot back on the cushions. "It's fine. I don't have the right to ask. I haven't even told you about myself."

When I try to put more space between us, Ryker grips my shoulder from where his hand rests on the back of the couch. And I shouldn't love his touch so much, after such a short time.

He loosens his grip and trails his fingers over my hair. "It's fine." But he removes his arm. "I can tell you about it."

"You don't have to tell me."

"I don't mind." He twists his mouth to the side and clasps his hands together. "My biological parents died when I was younger. My mom is actually my Aunt Gwen. She adopted me and my sister about ten years ago. It's just easier to call her Mom after everything. She's only a few years older than me, but she's been a role model for our family. And my friends. She's the ultimate mom."

"I'm glad you have her."

He nods as if it's an absentminded gesture. "Do you remember what I told you about Isobel's ex? How he cheated on her with a woman named Kizzy Kane?"

"Yeah."

He twiddles his thumbs. "My parents... were murdered. By Kizzy's mother."

I scoot closer until my thigh touches his. "Ryker, I'm so sorry."

"I've come to terms with it. Tinka's only recently learned about what happened to our parents. She's taking it hard, but she's dealing with it—"

The front door opens followed by the knock of the screen door against the threshold. "Ryker!"

His lips curl into a grin. "In her own way."

The blond girl from the festival struts into the room. "What are you doing?"

"Talking. Sharona, you haven't officially met her yet, but this is my sister Tinka."

She skips over to us. "Nice to meet you. Can I watch a movie?"

"Did you not hear me? We're talking in here."

"Fine. I'm asking Kieran if he can take me home."

"You can't leave. I'm babysitting you."

She props a hand on her hip. "I don't need a babysitter."

"Tinka."

She huffs. "I'll be outside. Come get me when you're done talking about the mushy stuff." She walks away, and the front door opens and shuts.

Ryker shakes his head. "She's such a drama queen."

"You're babysitting her?"

"Just while my mom and Cillian get settled with the baby. Our grandparents have Brendan and Ewan, but Tinka's older. She likes hanging out at the farm." He shrugs. "I don't mind having her around."

Rule One: Don't fall in love.

The most important rule flashes to the front of my mind. Saint and I would watch my mother "fall in love" with guy after guy. Almost like she hated being alone more than finding a guy with whom to spend her time.

Saint would nod toward her and the latest boyfriend. *Don't fall in love, Sharona. It's not worth it.*

But what if I found someone worth my time? If I found a love that was the furthest thing from what my mother calls love?

If I found a love so pure, it felt like a tragedy not to embrace it.

I curl my legs under me, getting comfy on the couch. "Isn't it exhausting?"

Ryker frowns. "What?"

"Saying yes all the time. Always being there for everyone when they need you."

"I don't mind."

"It's a lot of weight to carry."

He squeezes my knee. "I want people to know they can depend on me."

A deep breath flows out of me. "You're a good man."

His eyes burn into me like a brand. He brushes his thumb against my knee, and my pulse races at his touch. When he leans closer, I shift forward an inch. My breaths come out in sharp bursts until they're so loud I'm worried of making a fool of myself.

Ryker lowers his mouth, and his breath coasts over my parted lips. The old me would push him away, afraid of acting like my mom. But the new me wants to take this moment with both hands and not let go.

The door slams closed, and a few seconds later, Tinka storms in. I reel back, my pulse still thrumming.

She smacks her hand over her eyes. "Sorry, I didn't know y'all would be kissing."

Ryker groans and gets to his feet. "We're not kissing."

A part of me whines, wanting the moment back. Wanting Ryker to kiss me.

He frowns at his sister. "And why don't you pick a spot, either stay inside or outside."

I stand from the couch. "I better start on dinner."

Because I can't sit on the couch any longer, thinking about a kiss that never happened.

CHAPTER 18

• • • • ● • ● • • •

SHARONA

The soft breeze blows my hair as Ryker drives us to the diner. With the window rolled down, I try to focus on the fresh air rather than the man next to me in the truck.

Ryker drapes his wrist over the top of the steering wheel, completely at ease. The move, so masculine and confident, sends tingles along my body and disturbs the peace for which I'm searching.

Our almost-kiss last night flashes in my mind, and I crave what I didn't have.

Every moment I spend with Ryker pushes me closer to falling for him. I've never been in love. Never allowed myself to get close to a man. But Ryker isn't any other man.

He's my safe haven.

The diner's parking lot is full of vehicles for the dinner rush. Ryker parks his truck in an empty space to the side of the building.

He turns off the ignition. "I'm serious, Sharona. This is on the farm bill, so you're getting whatever you want off the menu."

The corners of my lips curl up. "I can cook for dinner. It's not a big deal."

"You're getting a break tonight, and I don't want you to bring it up again. Not that I don't love your cooking."

He winks at me, and heat rushes into my cheeks. For once, I understand the advantage of a man taking charge. When Ryker assumes responsibility, I don't have to. Which is strange and refreshing.

He opens his door, and I hurry to get out. We meet at the bed of his truck, and he places his hand on my back.

The conversations burst around me as Ryker ushers me inside the diner. Almost every table and booth is full. A few waitresses I haven't met yet scurry around the dining area. Grady waves as he passes us on his way to the kitchen.

Ryker and I walk to the end of the counter. An older woman stands at the register.

She closes the drawer and faces us. "What can I do for y'all?"

Ryker holds up a piece of paper. "I need a to-go order. After I add ours."

"I'll give y'all a minute. Be right back."

As she walks away, Ryker leans over the counter and reaches for a pen by the register.

"Now, what'll you have?" he asks.

"I don't know." I can't remember the last time I ate at a restaurant. Eating out was another rare occurrence for my family.

Ryker grabs the menu I'm eyeing and places it in front of me. "You like vegetables. Do you like them fried?"

"Why would you fry them? They're great the way they are."

"You won't be saying that once you try the fried mushrooms." He scribbles it on the paper. "Come on. Look at the menu so we can get this order started."

I fiddle with the corner of the plastic menu, overwhelmed with the options. "I'll just have a burger."

He flicks his hand through the air. "We can have burgers at home. Pick something else."

Home.

He called Fable Farms home. My home.

My body should not react so violently to that word, but thoughts of having a home with Ryker shake me to my very core.

I gave up my dreams of being a mom and a wife. If the best I could give my kids was a situation similar to mine, I didn't want to have any. And if the only men I could have were like the ones my mom brought around, I didn't want one.

But Ryker... He would give me a great life. He would be a great husband. Caring. Protective.

Safe.

He dips his head at the menu, hopefully oblivious to the thoughts billowing in my mind. "What about chicken fried steak?"

My stomach growls, liking that choice.

Ryker laughs and writes it on the paper. "Sounds like that's a winner. I'll get that, too. Mashed potatoes and green beans, okay?"

I nod.

His eyes narrow. "They also have broccoli, squash, gumbo—"

"I'll have that." Okra gumbo is one of my favorites.

He grins as he writes it on the piece of paper.

"What?"

He finishes writing and replaces the pen by the register. "I'm just glad you're telling me what you want." His smile widens. "We like similar things."

I need a breather. "Is there a bathroom?"

He jerks his head behind me. "Through there."

I take off for the restroom, ignoring the stares I get from some of the customers. By the time I shove through the door of the women's restroom, my body feels under attack from the connection building with Ryker.

My breath whooshes out of me as I clutch the sink counter. He draws me closer with every word, every action, every bit of goodness.

And when he called Fable Farms my home, it was like my life slotted into place. Like a key inserting into a locked door, allowing me access to the one thing I've wanted for so long.

To belong somewhere.

Hope blossoms like a flower ready for me to pick. Delicate and enticing. If only I'm prepared for the fallout if someone plucks it out of my hand.

When I exit the restroom, I check the people in the diner out of instinct.

And I freeze.

That can't be... They can't be here.

A woman with brown hair like mine sits in the corner of the diner across from a lanky man with a scowl.

My mom and Jimmy.

I stumble back into the restroom and lock myself in a stall. My breathing escalates as I sit on the toilet and wrap my arms around myself.

I should have known. My life is nothing more than one disaster after another. Even if I found a little good with Ryker, it won't last.

CHAPTER 19

• • • • • • • • • •

RYKER

My stomach knots as I check the time on my phone. Sharona's been in the restroom for twenty minutes. She wouldn't have tried to run away again, would she?

I look around the diner, trying to figure out if something or someone is out of place. A few strangers mixed in with the townsfolk. Nothing too bizarre.

As Liese deposits my order on the counter, the worries in my mind double.

Sharona fell in the restroom and is unconscious.

She sneaked out a window and ran away.

Someone kidnapped her.

"Liese, would you mind checking the bathroom for Sharona?"

"Sure," she says. "Is she okay?"

"I don't know. She's been gone for a long time."

"I'll be right back."

She walks away, and I work hard to quiet the fears shouting at me. But she returns a few seconds later, alone. My already jacked-up pulse spikes.

"She wouldn't come out of the stall," she says. "There's no one else in there, if you want to—"

Before she finishes, I march toward the women's restroom. I'll apologize for being rude later.

My knuckles rap on the door. "Sharona?" I wait for a response and knock again. "Sharona, I'm coming in."

I push open the door and face the three stalls in the small restroom. A pair of white sneakers peek out from the bottom of the left stall door.

"Sharona? Are you okay?"

Her feet shuffle toward the door. She unlocks it, opens it, and flings herself toward me.

I stumble back and catch her in my arms. A part of me loves the fact she's clutching me so tightly, but she's shaking.

My arms tighten around her shoulders. "You're okay."

Her forehead digs into my chest as she shields her face from me.

I run my hand over her long hair. "It's okay. I'm here."

She starts to sob.

I hold her, content to soothe her any way I can. This sweet brunette came to me when she could have pushed me away. The runaway girl who keeps everyone at a distance willingly ran into my arms.

In the middle of a diner restroom, I realize this woman has burrowed herself so deep into my life she's obliterated any future without her.

Time passes, and she eventually stops crying. Her tremors subside, and she relaxes into me. God must be watching because nobody enters the restroom while I'm inside, thank goodness.

Sharona sniffles and lifts her head. "I'm sorry. I didn't know what to do."

"You're fine. You want to tell me what's wrong?"

"I can't go out there."

"Tell me why."

"Not here. Can we leave?" She whimpers and presses into me. "We can't leave. They'll see me."

I brush my thumb across her cheek. "I'll sneak you through the kitchen and out the back."

Her hands fist my shirt. "Yes, please. Get me away from here."

She might as well be a princess locked in a tower, begging the prince to save her from dragons. And it makes me want her all the more.

My hand latches onto hers. "Don't let go, okay?"

"Wouldn't dream of it."

Her trust in me shoots adrenaline through my veins, bolstering my ego.

As I lead her out of the restroom, I shield her with my body, blocking her from view. We walk the short distance to the kitchen.

Grady looks at us as he flips a burger. "What are y'all doing?"

I shake my head. "I'll explain later."

When I pull Sharona through the back exit into the parking lot, her grip on my hand tightens. My focus fluctuates between the empty lot and the scared woman with me. I ensure she's safe as I lead her to my truck and open the passenger door.

She scrambles into the seat. "What about our food?"

"I'm gonna go back and get it. Will you be okay by yourself for a few minutes?"

"I'll be fine."

And because I can't help myself, I kiss her on the forehead. "Wait here." I shut her door and go through the back of the diner and enter the kitchen.

Grady steps into my path. "What's going on?"

"No clue. Sharona freaked, so I had to get her out through the back."

"Did someone say something to her?"

"I just said, I don't know. Let me figure it out, and I'll text you later."

He helps me grab the food from the dining area and follows me to my truck. As we set the bags of food on my back seat, I check on Sharona.

"You okay, beautiful?"

She's curled into herself, staring out the window behind a curtain of her hair. But she manages a nod.

Grady pats my shoulder and heads back inside.

I shut the back door and rush around the hood. Once I'm in the truck and at Sharona's side, my body settles. "Ready?"

"Yes," she says. "Get me away from here. Please."

CHAPTER 20

· · · • ● • ● • · ·

SHARONA

Instead of taking the food to the main house, Ryker drives along the fence line. The truck dips into the ruts in the field and jostles us. When the quiet lasts too long, I break.

"Why aren't we going to the house?"

Ryker drums his thumbs on the steering wheel. "I want to show you something."

"But the food will get cold. Everyone's probably hungry by now."

"They'll be fine. We can reheat the food."

"Ryker—"

"This won't take long."

We pass an open pasture and empty fields where I assume they grow their crops. Ryker slows the truck to a stop near a brush line of trees.

He parks and turns off the ignition. "Here we are."

We both climb out of the truck. The blades of grass brush against my jeans as I meet Ryker by the tailgate.

He drops it and pats the top. "Hop up."

We settle side by side on the tailgate. Fable Farms slopes below us, spanning the vast fields. The breeze rustles the leaves on the trees and the dry grass. The clouds roll over the sun, dimming its rays. And the turn of the fall season comforts me like the shelter of Ryker's jacket.

He scans our surroundings. "I love coming out here. I can be alone and get out of my head for a bit. Helps me when I need to think."

"It's a great place."

He interlaces his fingers with mine and lifts our hands. "Is this okay?"

"Yes."

Our hands fall onto my lap as he looks away.

"Aren't you going to ask me what happened back at the diner?"

"You'll tell me when you're ready," he says. "I'm okay with waiting."

I bite my lip. He's done enough waiting. He's given me so much of himself, and I'm ready to give a little in return.

"I saw my mom."

"Okay..."

"She was with her boyfriend."

Ryker's eyes bore into me before they narrow. "Was he the one who hurt you?"

I suck in a breath. "How did you figure that out so fast?"

"I can connect the dots." He releases my hand and jumps off the tailgate. He stomps away and clasps his hands behind his head. After a moment, he returns to me. "What did he do?"

I lean back. "We don't have to talk about it."

"I'm not mad at you, Sharona. I *won't* be mad at you."

How does he always know what to say, how best to soothe me?

He pushes my knees apart and steps between them so they're bracketing his hips. His hands slide to my waist. "You're safe here."

With his face close to mine, my brain locks on his proximity and convinces me to talk about my home life.

"My mom's had lots of boyfriends," I say, my voice a whisper. "Some were okay, some weren't. Some got angry, some left me alone."

Ryker's thumb brushes against my hip, but he remains quiet. Listening as I disclose the past I've kept hidden.

"My brother Saint protected me. He died two years ago from a drug overdose. He wasn't an addict. He took me with him to a party, away from our mom and her boyfriend. The party got out of hand. I didn't know what had happened, what he had done, until the next morning." A tear trails down my face. "He was my big brother."

Ryker nods as if he understands my pain. As if he's here to endure it with me.

"I'm sorry I didn't tell you," I say. "It's been hard, without him. Not just because he's gone, but I've had to deal with my mom's boyfriends on my own."

Ryker squeezes me as if he knows I need his strength. "What happened?"

"Her new boyfriend tried to..." I clutch his arm. "I fought him off as much as I could, but he knocked me around for refusing him. He said he'd finish with me when my mom went to bed. I shut myself in my room, packed my things, and crawled out the window."

"Smart move," Ryker says. "I'm proud of you."

A thread of warmth spirals inside me. "She hasn't made the best choices, but she's still my mom. It wasn't always bad."

His arms tighten around me. "Do you want to go back?"

"Not really. I miss my mom, but... this is my home now."

"I'm happy to hear that."

Without my worries and past between us, this moment collides into focus. How Ryker's holding me, how we're wrapped in each other, how close I am to a man.

How safe and treasured I feel with him.

"I'm too fragile, Ryker. One wrong move, and I'm worried I'll fall apart."

His hand shifts to my cheek. "Then you fall apart. And I'll be there with you."

He closes the distance between us and presses his mouth to mine. I close my eyes as sparks erupt inside me, lighting my body on fire. He tilts my head and deepens the kiss. My fingers clench his arm as I follow his lead and savor this moment.

The moment I finally get what I want.

The moment I let a man in.

Ryker breaks away, and I almost shove caution aside and tug him back for another kiss.

A breath falls from his lips as he winds his arms back around my waist. "If you ever need this place, you let me know. I'll drive you out here as fast as I can."

So willing to help. So willing to protect. Nobody has cared this much about me in a long time.

And as he steals another kiss, I give him all of myself and trust he won't break my heart.

CHAPTER 21

· · · ● · ● · ● · · ·

RYKER

When Isobel's brothers Ward and Rand laugh their way to the house with soaked clothes, I find myself doubting the decision to ask her family for help.

Kieran scuffs each of them on the back of the head. "Stop fooling around and get to work."

Stephen sighs from his perch on the porch. "I hate this. I wish I could help more."

"We're fine," I say from my spot in the yard. "And you help plenty even though you're down one arm."

He clomps down and heads to the henhouse.

My shirt constricts my movement as I rotate my shoulders. Is this fabric tighter than usual? Have I gained weight? Not surprising, since I take second helpings of Sharona's cooking.

The screen door shuts behind me. Aunt Anna walks across the porch with a frown. "The numbers are good, but y'all are working too hard. We need to hire more help."

While my friends and I handle the manual labor on the farm, my great-aunt manages the business side of Fable Farms with the help of my stepdad. Though she does most of the work at home, she comes out occasionally to work in the office.

I rub the back of my neck. "Yeah, I know. We'll ask around and see if we can get some new hires."

"I'll look, too. I'll try to come in again next week."

"Thanks. Have a good Thanksgiving."

As she drives away, the front door opens again.

Sharona walks onto the porch and stops on the top step. "Hi."

Our kiss yesterday hasn't made her any less shy. All day I've tried to get her alone, and either I've been busy or she has.

But we're both free now.

I plant myself on the step below hers. "I thought you were at Blake's."

"I asked Genevieve to bring me back in time for dinner. I thought I'd make extra food to feed everyone since Isobel's family is here."

She's too sweet.

"Yo, lovebirds!" Ward says.

Sharona jerks back, putting space between us. I hadn't even realized I was leaning toward her.

I scowl at the fourteen-year-old who laughs along with his twin brother.

My attention shifts back to the gorgeous woman in front of me. "Unfortunately, they're always like this. You'll have to get used to them."

Tires scrunching over our dirt road alert me to a visitor. Wanting Sharona to stay with me, I take her hand and lead her off the porch.

She tugs on my sleeve. "I need to start dinner."

"Later."

I give her a peck, and she blushes.

A small black car rolls to a stop next to our vehicles. Isobel joins Kieran and the twins a few feet away as Stephen walks out of the henhouse.

He looks at each of us. "Nobody was going to warn me Liv would be showing up?"

"I thought it would be best to delay the inevitable," Isobel says. "That way you ration your arguments."

His eyes lock on Liv's car. "She's going to be helping on the farm with the twins and Thatcher?"

Isobel walks toward the parked car. "That's the plan."

He mutters in Spanish and runs a hand through his hair.

After Isobel's family greets Liv, I give her a hug. She's wearing her typical dark clothes, from her gray T-shirt and leather jacket to the ripped jeans and combat boots. Her wavy hair, typically dyed with some color, has a few blue strands mixed in with the black.

When she looks at Stephen, she bristles.

A smile crosses his face. "Olivia."

She glares. "Santos."

Isobel's cousin Liv McKellar was friends with Stephen's older sister Mary. That close friendship had no impact on Stephen and Liv's attitudes toward each other. They argue whenever they're together. Stephen says she's overly indignant and needs to lighten up. Liv calls him an arrogant flirt who takes his jokes too far.

Hoping to cut the tension, I clear my throat. "Liv, this is Sharona."

Liv stays locked in on Stephen before giving the woman next to me her attention. "Nice to meet you."

"You too," Sharona says.

As everyone talks with each other, I pull Sharona off to the side.

"We're going to let Liv know what she can help with for the next few days."

"Do you want me to stay with you?" she asks.

Yes, I do. Dinner can wait.

"What did you just say?" Liv yells.

Stephen laughs as she shoves him. They start bickering, and Isobel tries to keep the peace. Her brothers take off with Kieran, though the twins chuckle and look at Stephen and Liv over their shoulders.

Perhaps Sharona should escape into the kitchen. She needs time to get to know Liv before she has to tolerate her and Stephen's constant arguing.

I sigh. "I better join them. I'll see you in a few for dinner."

"Allegra's supposed to be here soon to help me with a new recipe."

She and Allegra have bonded over their mutual love of cooking. We've reverted back to sandwiches for lunch, but Sharona does a lot to fix us a home-cooked meal for supper.

"Can't wait." I pull her closer and bend my head to meet her gaze. "I'm about to kiss you, so prepare yourself."

She relaxes against me. "Go for it."

The small glimpse at her carefree attitude snaps me into action. I surge forward and press my lips to hers. She leans into me and wraps her arms around my neck.

I pull back only to give her one more peck. "I'll see you later."

Then I force myself to walk away before I'm tempted to blow the whole day kissing her.

The sun sets as I walk into the house and toss my ripped shirt onto the floor. I should have figured out what was wrong when I felt how tight my clothes were earlier. If Stephen keeps shrinking my clothes, I'm enlisting Kieran for some retaliation. Maybe we'll toss his clothes in the chicken coop.

I take a step toward my room and stop. The scents of chicken and garlic drift down the hall, and my stomach growls.

After I remove my work boots, I stroll to the kitchen. Should I get a shirt right now? Maybe. Do I want to show off for Sharona? No doubt.

When I reach the kitchen, I heave a sigh and prop my shoulder against the wall.

Sharona stands at the stove, a cute apron tied around her waist. I soak in every part of her, from the bun on top of her head to her bare feet.

I would give up the farm if I could come home to this—to Sharona—every night.

As she removes a spoon from the pot, her head snaps in my direction. She screams and throws the spoon. It misses me and lands at my feet.

A breath puffs out of her. "You scared me." She glances at my bare torso and turns around. "Where's your shirt?"

"It ripped."

"Again?"

"Yep. Stephen must be bored. I came in to get a new one."

"You won't find one in the kitchen."

I smile at the back of her head, loving this confident side of her. "What are you cooking?"

She peeks over her shoulder. "I'll tell you when you put on a shirt."

I run a hand through my hair, flexing my bicep. "Where's Allegra?"

Sharona's eyes flick to my arm, and my lips twitch. She may still be a skittish little bunny, but she's not hating the view.

Her cheeks turn red, and she faces the stove. "She left already. I told her I didn't need her to finish up."

"Finish up what?"

"Put a shirt on first."

Deciding I've teased her enough, I push off the wall. "I'll be right back. But know you bruise my ego when you don't give me any attention."

Her faint giggle follows me as I leave the room. After I put on a white T-shirt, I walk back into the kitchen. Sharona removes a baking sheet from the oven and places it on the stove. Breaded chicken sizzles on the pan.

I step behind her and snake my arm around her waist. She stiffens before leaning back against me.

I drag my nose down her neck. "You smell good."

She shivers. "It's from cooking."

"Hmm, don't know about that."

"Did you put a shirt on? I can't tell."

"Reach behind you and see for yourself."

She shakes her head. "The heat from the kitchen is enough. I can't deal with yours."

I chuckle. "Will you tell me what you're making now?"

She slips off the oven mitts and places them on the counter. "Chicken and pasta with a lemon garlic butter sauce."

"Butter? Wait, pasta?"

She lifts her hand. "Hear me out. We cooked gluten-free noodles. I used gluten-free bread crumbs, so the chicken's all good. The sauce has lemon, garlic, salt, and butter, but Allegra brought the butter Isobel can have. It should all be good with her allergies."

By the time she finishes explaining, she has a big smile on her face. Like she's so proud of herself and happy about what she created.

I grab her hand and give it a squeeze. "This is amazing. Thank you."

"It's not a problem. I was excited to make it."

"It means a lot that you went to all this trouble. And it sounds delicious. I can't wait to try it."

She pulls her hand away and busies herself with a bowl of broccoli. "I just have to finish up the veggies, then it'll be ready.

I lean back against the center table. "I should have known you'd be cooking vegetables."

"They're good for you. Expect them at every meal."

I watch her as she works. She doesn't seem to mind that I planted myself in the kitchen. When she passes by, I grab her apron and tug her to me.

She sighs. "I'm not going to be able to finish dinner if you keep distracting me."

Fully intent on distracting her, I cradle her face in my palms. She raises herself on her tiptoes and meets me halfway. My lips press against hers, and she kisses me back. I wind my arms around her waist, holding her closer. She relaxes in my arms, and our kiss slows like we're moving through water.

Unhurried.

Languid.

Like soft waves pulling me under, trapping me in a daze.

"Y'all want to take this to a different room?"

Sharona wrenches herself free from me. I glare at Stephen's smiling face.

He holds up his hand. "Just be glad I found you and not the twins. They'd show no mercy."

I blow out a breath and push off the table. "Dinner's about done. Can you grab the others?"

"Sure." He spins around and grins at us over his shoulder. "Don't burn the food."

He walks away, and I turn to Sharona. Though I want to take his advice and move my make out session with her to another room, everyone will be here soon to eat dinner.

And my girl deserves to have her meal appreciated.

I shove my hands in my pockets to keep from touching her. I can only control myself so much.

She pats her cheeks. "I can't believe that just happened. It's so embarrassing. Is he angry we were kissing in the kitchen?"

"He was just teasing us. Don't worry about it."

She nods but wrings her hands.

Her confidence from earlier has disappeared, and I want it back. I want the girl who lets me flirt with her even if it's out of her comfort zone. Who lets the world fade out of focus when I tease her because she can't stop blushing.

"I'll give you some space," I say. "If I stay in here any longer, my hands will start wandering, then we're bound to get into trouble."

She smiles as if I gave her what she wanted. "As long as I'm with you, I think I could handle a little trouble."

Same here, beautiful. Same here.

CHAPTER 22

. . . ● ● . ● ● . .

SHARONA

AMOS PLOPS DOWN NEXT to me on the couch. "Have you ever played video games?"

I smile at the cute eight-year-old. He asks me the most interesting questions.

Blake invited me to his house before Ryker takes me to his mom and stepdad's house for Thanksgiving dinner. Genevieve and I have been chatting for the past hour while I wait for Ryker to finish his work around the farm.

"I have," I say. "My brother had some video games when we were younger." Of course, that was before my mom sold them to get money for drugs and alcohol.

Amos nods. "I bet I'd beat you."

Genevieve steps toward the couch, holding two mugs. "Amos, don't be rude."

I shake my head. "It's the truth. He probably would."

She offers me a mug. "Careful. The tea's hot."

"Thanks," I say, taking it from her.

She sits on the other side of me. "Amos, your dad's looking for you."

The boy scowls. "You just want me to leave, so y'all can have girl talk."

"Is that what your father says?"

He shrugs and walks out of the room.

She tucks her feet beneath her and cradles her own mug. "Sorry about that. My brother does a great job raising them, but I think they miss out on a woman's touch."

"It's fine." Hanging out with Harding and Amos has soothed some of the hurt inside me. It's like having a brother again, only this time I get two.

Steam rises from the top of my mug, and I blow on the tea to cool it. "It's sweet of your brother to let you crash here."

"Yeah, it's been great since I've been back."

Her definition of great must be different than mine. She looks drained, and her eyes are puffy.

"Are you feeling okay?" I ask.

"Of course. It's Thanksgiving, and I get to spend it with my family and friends. Why wouldn't I be happy?"

"I don't know. I'm just checking."

Her gaze falls as she takes a sip of her tea. "I'm fine. Just thinking about... some stuff." Before I can probe further, she nudges my knee with her foot. "So, how's the boyfriend?"

I bite my lip to curb my smile. "Ryker's not my boyfriend."

"Sure seems like he is. What with all the kissing and how he doesn't leave you alone for long."

Warmth spreads through my cheeks. "We haven't put any labels on it or really talked about anything."

"I say take control and get what you want." She reaches over and checks her phone. "When did you say he was picking you up?"

"About five."

"Well, I don't know why I bothered with tea. He's going to be here any minute."

We discuss some of the recipes I've found and the progress of the inn's remodeling.

After a couple of minutes, I check my phone. "It's five ten. I don't have any texts or calls from him. Should I be worried?"

"No, we'll wait a bit longer. He's probably almost here."

But when five thirty rolls around, I've finished my tea, and Ryker hasn't shown up.

I fidget with my phone. "Do you think something happened to him?"

"Why don't you call him?" Genevieve asks.

"I don't want to seem clingy."

"He's thirty minutes late. You have every right to call him."

As I debate whether or not to call Ryker, the sound of tires outside reaches the living room. I rush to the window and peek through the curtain. Ryker's truck pulls up to the house.

"He's here."

Genevieve stands from the couch. "Maybe something came up."

I follow her to the front door, and she opens it.

Ryker jogs up the steps and stops in front of us. "Sorry, I'm late."

Genevieve huffs next to me.

I ignore her. "Are you okay?"

He presses his lips together. "Yes. I'm sorry."

"It's fine. I was just worried. You sure you're okay?"

He expels a deep breath and runs his hand through his blond curls. "Yeah, I just... forgot."

Genevieve gasps, and I take a step back.

Ryker's face scrunches. "I know it's terrible, and I'm sorry. I was caught up on the farm, and then Stephen got a call, saying his dad had a heart attack. I didn't want him driving by himself, especially with Boaz, so I offered to drive him. We were halfway down the lane when I remembered I was going to pick you up. I dropped them off with Kieran and rushed right over."

My mind struggles to comprehend the words flowing out of his mouth.

He has a reason for being late. I won't let it get me down. Everything is fine.

"How's Mauricio doing?" Genevieve asks.

"He's stable," Ryker says.

He has a reason. He has a reason...

I want to cling to logic, but my mind shouts that I wasn't important to Ryker. "I need a minute."

Before I question where I'm going, I walk out of the house and end up in the passenger seat of Ryker's truck. I drop my head into my hands, the past few minutes reminding me of how it feels to be back at my mom's.

Forgettable.

Insignificant.

Unwanted.

I can't go back to a place where that's acceptable.

The driver's side door opens, and someone climbs in. The door shuts, pulling silence into the cab.

"I got your phone," Ryker says. "You left without it."

My fingers clench around my forehead.

He grabs my wrists and pries my hands away from my face. "Sharona?"

Tears form in my eyes. The man I hoped I could count on forgot about me. Instead of giving me happiness, he gave me pain.

I lean toward the window, trying to put space between us. Ryker doesn't let me.

He reaches for my waist and tugs me into the middle of the bench seat. "Please don't be upset. I'm truly sorry. It all happened so fast."

The tears trail down my face. "It's Thanksgiving, and you forgot about me. How do you expect me to feel?" I raise my hand. "And I realize that you were helping a friend, but can you see where I'm coming from?"

"It didn't mean anything. I just forgot. I have a lot of things on my mind."

"And I'm obviously not one of them."

He winces. "Don't say that. It was..." He rubs his thumb against my back. "I'm sorry. I don't want this to ruin your day."

My heart splinters inside of my chest. Maybe Ryker doesn't like me as much as I thought. Or as much as I like him.

He slides his hand down my thigh. "Let me make it up to you."

"How?"

"Let's go out tomorrow night. Just you and me."

I wipe my cheeks. "Like... a date?"

He smiles. "Yes. I think it's about time."

"You can't just ask me out after you messed up. I don't want a pity date."

"It's not a pity date. I've wanted to go out with you for a while."

The wound of being forgotten still festers, but I want to go on a date with him.

He cocks his head. "So what do you say? Would you go out with me?"

I shelve the hurt to analyze later. "I don't have anything to wear."

"I'll ask Isobel if you can borrow some of her clothes."

"For the record, I've never been on a date. I've never really felt comfortable enough to be alone with a boy. And Saint scared off a few." I shrug. "Big brothers."

Ryker squeezes my knee. "I'm honored to be your first date, baby."

His words along with him calling me *baby* have me seconds away from spontaneously combusting.

He kisses my temple. "Buckle up, so I can take us home, beautiful."

There he goes again, calling Fable Farms my home.

The last time he said that, I was relieved to find a place where I belonged. But after what happened today, I'm scared of hoping for a permanent home. Because part of me believes it's not possible, and I'll soon be on my own once again.

CHAPTER 23

· · · · ● · ● ● · · ·

RYKER

THE NEXT MORNING, I walk into the kitchen and find Isobel leaning against the counter.

She lifts her mug. "Just brewed a pot of coffee."

"You're a lifesaver." I pour myself a cup.

Kieran props himself in the kitchen threshold. "Any news from Stephen?"

Isobel shakes her head. "He's hopefully getting some rest."

Kieran dips his head toward her mug. "Don't drink too much, Is. You had mushrooms and tomatoes last night. I don't want your histamine levels to get too high."

"I know," she says. "I won't finish this."

We walk to the living room. Kieran and Isobel sit on the couch, and I take the armchair.

Isobel sets her mug next to her. "Stephen will probably be at the hospital all day. It can't be easy for him. He has the farm and now he and Esther will have to help Tina figure out what to do at the clinic for a few days."

I take a sip of my coffee. "And with his injury and taking care of Boaz, his life just keeps getting more demanding. I was trying to think of what we could help with."

Kieran props his boot on the coffee table. "I don't want to sound insensitive, but we have our plates full too."

"Maybe Sharona could cook some meals for his family," Isobel says. "We could buy extra ingredients and double what we normally make."

"I don't want to volunteer her for anything until I ask her," I say.

"Of course. Liv's coming over soon, and I'll ask her if she can help around more."

After we talk for a few minutes, Isobel and Kieran take off to start working. I linger in the living room as long as I can, wanting to see Sharona before I get my day started.

The front door opens, and I stand from the chair. Liv emerges from the hall, dressed in her normal dark clothes and combat boots.

She fidgets with some of the dyed strands in her hair. "Hey, Ryker."

"Morning."

"Did Isobel let you know I'd be coming to help?"

"She did. And thanks."

"No worries. I just need to use the restroom real quick." She disappears down the hall.

Sharona's closed door feels like a canyon keeping me from the woman on the other side. Maybe work can wait a few more minutes.

Stephen walks through the front door with his signature hat and belt buckle missing. He runs his hand through his curly hair before he rubs his arm.

I place my mug on a side table. "Hey, what are you doing here? Shouldn't you be at the hospital?"

He scratches his head. "I will, I just... last night was a lot. I needed to do something physical to reset."

"Where's Boaz?"

"Blake's at the henhouse, and he said he'd watch him for a bit."

The bathroom door opens, and Liv struts out. Stephen stares at her as she stumbles to a stop. Neither one offers an insult or a jab.

Stephen swallows hard. "Hey."

Liv shuffles on her feet. "Hi."

A weird sensation settles over the room like a morning fog. Usually these two would be at each other's throats right now, fighting for the last word before they go their separate ways.

But it's as if they're unsure of how to act around each other.

Stephen takes a step forward. "I didn't know you'd be here."

Liv messes with her bracelet as if she can't keep still. "Yeah, Isobel wanted me to come over for a bit, so my dad dropped me off before heading to the firehouse."

"It's good to—" Stephen's eyes flash to me, and he backs toward the door. "Anyway, I'll be outside for a while if you need anything."

I lift my hand. "Wait, hold on. Liv, could you give us a second?"

"Of course," she says.

She and Stephen share another look as she passes him on her way out of the house.

With one of the awkward parties gone, I focus on Stephen and his family. "How's your dad?"

He shrugs. "He's fine. My mom spent the night there, and she's been keeping us updated. Isobel's coming with me to the hospital later."

"Is there anything I can do?"

"No. It's a waiting game, and all we do is sit and worry. Isobel's just keeping me company."

"I wish I could, too, but Sharona and I are going out tonight."

"Ah," he says. "I see how it is. A few weeks with a pretty girl, and your friends come in second place."

I wave him off. "Get out of here."

He snorts and heads toward the door.

"Hey, Santos."

He glances at me over his shoulder.

"We're here if you need anything," I say. "And we're going to help your family out with meals, so y'all don't have to worry about food."

"Thanks, man."

He leaves, and I take my mug to the kitchen and place it in the dishwasher. I pass by Sharona's door and scuff my boots against the floor, hoping it wakes her up. When I realize what I'm doing, I shake my head.

I'm an idiot. Causing a ruckus to wake up a girl.

After what happened yesterday, I need to be more aware of my actions. Sharona might have agreed to go on a date with me, but she's still looking for me to prove myself.

Which means I have to be on my very best behavior.

CHAPTER 24

· · · · ● · ● · ● · ·

SHARONA

I REST MY BACK against the door as footsteps pass by. The front door opens then shuts. The silence feels even louder than the conversations on which I eavesdropped.

Ryker wishes he could be here tonight instead of on a date with me?

If he didn't have to worry about me, he could help his friends and spend time with his family. Though I want him to consider me a priority, I don't want to be a hassle or an inconvenience. I can't force him to choose between his family and me if it hurts him.

I grab my phone and dial Genevieve's number.

"Hello?" she says.

"It's Sharona."

"Hey, what's up?"

"Can I stay with you and Blake for a few days?"

Blake's house is on Fable property, but it'll have to be far enough. I can't afford to go anywhere else.

Genevieve pauses. "I'm sorry, can you repeat that?"

"I need to move into a different house. Today. Now."

"Mm-hmm," she says as the clinking of dishes floats through the background. "May I ask why?"

"Can I explain later?"

Another pause. "Okay. Let me call you back."

We end the call, and I stuff all my things into my duffel. Living out of a bag means packing takes less than a minute. My mind runs rampant until Genevieve's name pops up on my phone.

I answer her call. "Hello?"

"My brother says you can stay with us for a few days."

A deep exhale puffs out of me. "Are you sure?"

"Of course," she says. "It'll be a bit crowded, but if it's only for a few days, we can manage."

That gives me a few days to figure out another plan. I'll look for a new place, a new job, and move somewhere I'm not a burden or a bother to anyone.

"Do you want me to come pick you up?" Genevieve asks.

"If you wouldn't mind."

"I'll be right there."

I hang up and put the room back the way I found it. I can't leave my mark on this place.

Which means stepping away from a relationship with Ryker.

My throat constricts as I scroll to our messages and see the one he sent me last night. A goodnight text where he called me beautiful again.

I shake my head and type out a quick text, canceling our date and telling him I need time to think. After I hit send, I take my duffel bag onto the porch and sit on the top step. My knee bounces as I wait for Genevieve. Hopefully everyone's too busy to notice her car.

Less than two minutes later, she pulls up to the main house. I book it to her car and throw myself along with all my stuff into the passenger seat.

"Are you okay?" she asks.

"Drive, please. I'll explain at your brother's house."

She doesn't pry as she drives me away from my home.

Because it was my home.

It was more than a house. I belonged there. But I should have known it would be too good to be true.

Genevieve squeezes my hand. "Are you sure you don't want to talk to him?"

When she brought me to Blake's house, I had to tell her what I heard Ryker say to Stephen and why I wanted to leave. She said maybe I misheard or misunderstood, but it didn't change my decision. A relationship with Ryker wouldn't work.

I shift further into the couch cushions. "I'm sure."

She presses her lips together. "I appreciate you talking to me. And I won't spread your business. About Ryker or your home life."

Crying made me vulnerable. When I was in tears, I confided in her. What could it hurt? I'd already told Ryker, and that was a bust. I wanted to trust someone again, so I told her why I ran away from my mom's house weeks ago.

Amos enters the living room and walks over to me. "My dad said you're staying with us."

"Yes. I hope that's okay."

"Sure, but we don't have any extra beds."

Genevieve clicks her tongue. "Amos, stop. Go away." She pats my arm. "We have a spare air mattress, and you can bunk in here with me."

Amos walks into the kitchen, leaving Genevieve and me alone on the couch.

My phone rings, and I look at the screen. "He's calling me."

"Answer it," she says.

"No, I can't. I texted him. That should be enough."

My phone stops ringing but chimes as a text comes through. I flip my phone over on my lap to hide the message.

Genevieve's phone rings, and she reaches for it on the end table.

"Is it him?" I ask. "Don't let him know what happened."

Her mouth turns down at the corners before she drops her phone face down on the cushions next to her. "It's not him."

Her voice sounds all wrong. Monotone and sullen. Genevieve reminds me of the sun, all bright and in your face. In a good way, of course. But today, clouds have rolled in and covered her cheery attitude.

"Is everything okay?" I ask.

"No, but I'm trying to figure it out."

My fingers clench my phone as it rings again. "Do you want to talk about it?"

She stands and swipes her hands through the air. "No. Let's make a rule."

Rules? I can do rules.

"While you're here," she says, "let's not talk about men, okay?"

So her problem is with a man. I try to think if I've seen her with anyone in particular, but she interacts with people every day.

She pulls me to my feet. "Now let's get cooking. Something tells me it'll make you feel better."

CHAPTER 25

• • • • • • • • • •

RYKER

THE CHICKENS IN MY path squawk and scatter as I stride to the barn. I grab the first thing I see—a shovel—and toss it as far as I can.

Kieran's brows slam together. "What's your problem?"

"Nothing."

"Is it relationship trouble?"

"I said it's nothing."

"Women like it when you apologize."

I prop my hands on my hips. "What makes you think I messed up?"

"Because you messed up last time."

"Yeah, well, not this time." I blow out a breath and hang my head. "It's been three days, and Sharona's still avoiding me."

After she canceled our date Friday, she sent me a short text saying she moved into Blake's house. She's ignored all my calls and texts. Blake is as clueless as I am, and Genevieve knows but won't tell me. Either way, they're not helpful.

Kieran removes his work gloves. "You could just stop by the house."

"I'm not going to show up where I'm not wanted."

He passes me and claps me on the shoulder. "Just don't let your temper give me extra work."

He drives away on a four-wheeler, and I walk to the porch to cool off. Stephen sits in one of the chairs, staring out at the farm.

I sit in the chair next to him. "You going to the hospital soon?"

"Yeah," he says, "I just wanted to let Boaz get some energy out before we left."

I follow his gaze to Liv who's propped Boaz on her hip. They're by the cows, trying to get close enough to pet them.

"You let Liv take him?" I ask.

"She offered to watch him so I could have a break. Pretty considerate, right?"

"Yeah, that's... different."

He shifts in his chair. "Any word from Sharona?"

"No. What bothers me is not knowing what I did. I wish she'd talk to me." I lean forward and clasp my hands together. "I can't lose her."

"I get it," he says.

When he looks back at Liv, my eyes narrow. This softer edge is strange. But whatever happened between him and Liv, he obviously doesn't want to talk about it.

I get to my feet. "I'm going to call her again."

As I walk inside the house, I pull out my phone and dial Sharona's number.

No answer.

I shoot her a text and wait.

No answer.

My fingers clench my phone. I've given her three days, and she's given me nothing. No response, no explanation. No chance to fix whatever happened.

No respect for our relationship.

Feeling desperate, I take Kieran's advice.

Ryker:

If you don't call me back, I'll be at Blake's house in less than a minute.

Maybe showing up at Blake's will be the push she needs. Or at the very least, telling her I'm on my way will hopefully get her to answer.

Sure enough, she calls.

I answer before the first ring ends. "Sharona—"

"Don't come to Blake's house," she says, her voice firm. "I don't want to see or talk to you."

I prop myself against the back of the couch. "And you won't even tell me why? I can't make anything better if I don't know what I did."

"You can't fix this."

"Don't be so sure."

She huffs. "I can't do this. Leave me alone."

"Not until you tell me what's going on."

"Ryker, please."

"You can't keep running away from everything in your life."

"That's not..."

"And I deserve the respect of an explanation."

She pauses. "Fine. What do you want to talk about?"

"I'm not doing this over the phone." Forget empty threats. I'll drive the few acres and force her to talk to me if she won't willingly do it.

She sighs, long and tired. "Fine. Let's get this over with."

Don't know what that means. "I'm on my way."

As soon as she hangs up, I rush out the front door.

Isobel strolls out of the henhouse. "I thought you were helping me."

"Check the chickens yourself."

"You've been spending too much time with Kieran. His grumpy attitude is rubbing off on you."

"Sharona called. I'm heading to Blake's."

Her scowl smooths into a smile. "Say no more. You're done for the day."

I kiss her cheek on my way to my truck. My blood pumps faster as I turn the ignition. My body vibrates with the rumble of my truck, and I drive through the property with one task in mind.

Convincing Sharona to come home with me.

When I pull up to Blake's house, Sharona's sitting on the steps outside. Her arms are wrapped around her legs, and her chin rests on her knees.

She stands as I put my truck in park. I get out and slam my door. My emotions from the past three days throw me into dangerous territory as I march toward her.

I stop in front of her, and she flinches. My mind shouts to rein in my temper, but adrenaline courses through every part of my being.

For days, I've been worried sick as I tried to figure out how to reach her. She should know what she's put me through.

"Today is a weekday," I say. "You're supposed to be at the farm making lunch. Or did you forget the agreement we had when you came here."

We both wince at my words and my tone, but I can't find the mindset to put a lid on my boiling frustration.

Sharona crosses her arms. "I'm sorry, but I'm not coming back. You'll have to find someone else."

"I don't want someone else. I want you."

"I can be easily replaced."

My irritation lowers to a simmer. "Not to me, you can't. I thought we were on the same page."

"I could never be with a man who blames me."

The fire flickers out of me. "Blame you? What are you talking about?"

She straightens her back. "I heard you tell Stephen that you wished you could help him Friday night instead of going on a date with me."

"What? No, that's... I didn't mean..." I take a step toward her. "This is what you've been thinking this whole time?"

"Stephen said he felt like second place," she says. "I didn't want to come between you and your friends."

"He was joking. He knows how I feel about you. Or at least some of it." I close the distance between us and grab her hand. "I wish you would have come to me sooner. I didn't mean for it to come out that way. I meant I wish I was there to help, but I was excited to go out with you."

She leans away from me as her eyes fill with tears.

I squeeze her hand. "You need to trust me, Sharona."

"I do."

"Then don't run away."

"I just went to another house. I'm still on the property."

"You know I'm not being literal."

Her foot scuffs against the ground. "I don't want to be a bother or an obligation to you."

"You are the best thing to ever happen to me."

She wipes a tear away. "I'm sorry."

I cup her jaw with my free hand. "If there's ever an issue, come talk to me. You have a problem, you let me know."

She squirms a bit then nods. "I will."

I guide her mouth to mine. She doesn't kiss me back right away. My guess would be she's still processing everything.

When I'm about to break away and give her space, she relaxes into me. My fingers sift through her long hair, and I deepen the kiss. Her hands slide up my chest, but she lets me take control. And I force myself to pull back before I get carried away.

I brush my thumb across her cheek. "You ready to come back home?"

She sighs. "Yes."

After she grabs her things, I take her back to my truck and drive her to Fable Farms.

Right where she belongs.

CHAPTER 26

· · · · ● · ● · · ·

SHARONA

WHEN I CALL ALLEGRA Thursday morning for recipe help, I expect her to answer my questions over the phone. Instead, she invites me over to Gwen and Cillian's house in the afternoon to go over recipes in person. She mentions her family is having dinner with Gwen's tonight.

And when I'm in the middle of refusing, she hangs up to call Gwen. The two friends conference call me a minute later and convince me to go to Gwen's house.

Blake drops me off on his way into town around four. As I enter the house, kids scatter in all directions. Allegra and Gwen lead me to the dining room. We sift through multiple cookbooks for an hour, searching for recipes to accommodate Isobel's allergies.

Allegra spins the cookbook around to me. "You could try this with almond milk. It shouldn't taste any different."

I write the gravy recipe down. "That's a good one."

Gwen sits in the chair next to me, holding Maureen in her arms. "Kip's got them all corralled into the living room."

I close the cookbook. "I think I have enough for now. I'll get out of your hair."

Allegra latches onto my arm. "Nonsense. Stay for a bit. We haven't talked about Ryker yet."

My eyes widen.

Gwen sighs. "We agreed to be subtle when we brought it up."

Allegra's grip tightens. "But she was about to leave. She needs to tell us how it's going."

My relationship with Ryker has teetered into a gridlock after what happened earlier this week. I moved back into the main house and returned to cooking meals, but we didn't go on our date. A part of me wonders if I'm too much work for him. If I have a problem I can't see yet.

You have a problem, you let me know.

Ryker's words blend with those from my past and bring rule seven to the front of my mind.

We only trust each other, Saint used to say. *If you ever have a problem, call me. We'll figure it out together.*

Saint was my rock. I could always count on him. For weeks, I've built walls of trust with Ryker. But what if these walls are too fragile, just waiting for the next time he fails me?

I look at Gwen. Ryker's mom.

No way am I talking about my relationship with her son.

She smiles. "It's okay. Ryker's probably told me more than you think."

Twelve-year-old Simeon strolls into the kitchen. "Mom, Louisa's fussy."

Allegra stands and points a finger at us. "I'll be right back. Wait for me to talk about this."

She follows her eldest son out of the room.

Gwen pats Maureen and rocks her. "Ryker said he told you about his parents. And that you've experienced loss. I'm sorry about your brother."

I fiddle with the pen in my hand. "Thank you."

She looks at the baby in her arms. "My brother was the best person I knew. For the longest time, I couldn't understand why he died. I still don't really."

Memories of Saint flood my mind, and I clench the pen tighter. "Yeah. My brother Saint was my best friend."

"It's hard losing someone you love. Especially if it's under tragic circumstances. Especially if he's been there for you your whole life."

Tears well in my eyes.

"It takes time to deal with the hurt," she says. "To not feel the grief whenever you think of what happened to him."

She understands. She lost her brother like I did, and that connection opens the cage my anger's been rattling.

I wipe a tear that flows down my cheek. "I don't know if I'll ever get past it."

"I used to think that way," she says. "But then I focus on all the happy memories, on everything good, and I hold onto that."

A list of everything my mother has done in the past couple of years drowns everything good in my mind.

My fingers curl into fists in my lap. "I would have more memories if my mom didn't drink or use."

Gwen nods. "And I'd have more memories if my brother hadn't been murdered. But the anger isn't worth holding a grudge. There's a purpose for everything. I wouldn't have Ryker or Tinka if my circumstances were different. While I wouldn't have wished for my brother to die, I'm grateful for the two children who made me a mother."

I pluck at my jeans around my knee. "How were you able to forgive the person who... killed your brother?" The words are hard to get out. I don't know how she was able to move past it.

"It took me awhile," she says. "I had to start small, forgive Verena's children first. And one day, I realized my anger and frustration were only making me miserable. I was giving her actions too much control over my life. It took a lot of prayer, but I gave it all to God."

My mom has caused me so much trouble. Can I really forgive her for what she's done?

Gwen tilts her head to the side. "If your brother, or let's say Ryker, did something terrible, would you forgive them?"

My brother, yes. Ryker... I don't know. My mind flashes to last week when he forgot about me on Thanksgiving. The wound is still painful on that one.

"When you love someone," Gwen says, "you forgive the hurtful things they do."

My phone vibrates in my pocket, and I pull it out. *Mom* flashes on the screen.

Since I left on my birthday, she's called and texted me a few times. I've ignored her messages and voicemails. Why would I want to talk to her, hear her ask me where I am, or possibly try to convince me to return to her house?

I had nothing there.

But Gwen's words swirl in my mind. She said to start small. Maybe that means a small conversation.

And for the first time in weeks, I answer my mom's phone call. "Hello?"

"Hello," a man says on the other line. "This is Ross Collins with the SAPD. We have a Marilyn Bennett here, and we were trying to reach her next of kin. Your number is on her favorites."

I lurch to my feet. "What? I mean, yes, that's my mom. Is she okay?"

Gwen stands as Allegra comes back into the kitchen.

"She was found unconscious outside of a bar," the man says. "She sustained minor injuries, but the hospital will need to run more tests. We're transporting her to Grapevine South Baptist."

"Yes... I mean, thank you. I'll be right there." After I hang up, I scramble into my coat. "My mom is in the hospital. I need to go see her."

Allegra gasps. "Of course. I'm so sorry."

"Should I call Ryker?" Gwen asks.

I shake my head, already fumbling to call him. "I'll do it." I dial his number and press the phone to my ear. It rings multiple times before going to Ryker's voicemail.

Tears break through my steady composure. When I hear the beep on the other line, I leave Ryker a short message about what happened with my mom. After I ask if he can call me back, I hang up.

"I'll give him a few minutes," I say.

Gwen sways with Maureen. "I wish I could go with you."

"Me, too," Allegra says.

"No," I say, "you stay with your families. Ryker can go with me."

Twenty minutes pass, and I'm still waiting. Staring at my phone and willing Ryker to call me back. I try to reach him one more time but get his voicemail again. That makes four unanswered calls. I hope he's okay.

But I can't wait any longer, so I dial a different number. "I'll call Blake."

Gwen presses her cellphone to her ear. "He's not answering my calls either. Let me try again."

My call connects to Blake. "Yeah?"

"Hey, it's Sharona. Are you still around town? Would you be able to pick me up from Gwen and Cillian's?"

"Yeah, I can be there soon. Is everything okay?"

"I'll explain when you get here."

"I'm leaving Honeycutt's, so I'll be there in a bit."

"Thanks."

When I hang up, Gwen frowns at her phone.

"This isn't like him," she says. "I'm starting to get worried."

Oh, great. Now I'm imagining Ryker lying unconscious somewhere on the farm or maybe in a car accident on the side of the road.

I tap my foot from where I stand by the front door. "Do you think he's hurt?" I would hate for something to happen to him because he was trying to get to me.

Allegra pats my arm. "Just worry about your mom. We'll let you know when we hear from Ryker."

I spin toward the table. "I need to get the rest of my stuff."

"Stop," she says. "We'll take care of it. You need to focus on your mom."

Blake's truck rumbles up to the house, and I fling the door open.

I glance over my shoulder. "Thank you, both. Sorry to run off like this."

Allegra shakes her head. "No, don't worry. Keep us updated."

I rush out of the house and hop into Blake's truck.

His brows furrow. "What's wrong?"

The tears from earlier reappear. Over the past few weeks, I've grown close to Genevieve and her family. But instead of calling my closest friend, I called Blake. I've pushed men away for so long, but my time in Mustang Cross has illuminated how much I've been wishing for a good man to trust. Blake's a good man, and I'm glad I can rely on him.

But the man I most want to be by my side isn't here.

A tear falls down my cheek. "My mom's in the hospital. Grapevine South Baptist. I need to get there fast."

Blake puts the truck into drive. "Then let's get going."

CHAPTER 27

· · · ● · ● · ● · · ·

RYKER

My body wages a war against my mind as I stare at Sharona's name displayed on my phone. I want to talk to her so badly, but the familiar jacked-up truck rolling to a stop outside the main house demands my attention.

I set my phone on the end table next to me. I can call Sharona back. She'll understand. Right now, Isobel's going to need all our support.

I storm out of the house and march down the porch steps. My body tenses like a soldier preparing for battle. Everything else fades away as I channel the pain from a few months ago into armor.

Isobel stops in her tracks a few feet from the truck. Her eyes widen, and Kieran plants himself in front of her. Stephen shuts the gate for the cows and walks our way.

And the three of us form a barrier between Isobel and the cheating dirtbag who broke her heart.

Garrett slides out of the truck and lumbers around the hood. As if we're all still friends and he's here for an afternoon chat.

He smirks. "Nice to see everyone."

Kieran crosses his arms. "Don't know what you're doing here, but you need to turn around and drive back the way you came."

Garrett shakes his head. "Same old Kieran."

I move between him and my friends. "Whatever you're here for, I'm sure it can be handled over the phone. You need to leave."

He looks past me. "I wanted to talk to Isobel in private."

Kieran steps to my side. "That's not going to happen."

Garrett keeps his gaze focused behind us. "Isobel?"

"I don't want to talk to you." Her voice is thin, and the strong woman she normally is has vanished.

"Come on, Is. I just—"

"Don't call her that," Kieran says. "You lost that privilege when you cheated on her."

Garrett scowls at him. "I came to talk to Isobel. Not you."

"Anything you want to say can be said in front of everyone here," Isobel says.

He stuffs his hands in his pockets. "I want to give us another chance."

Stephen scoffs. "You can't be serious."

"Deadly," Garrett says. "I don't want to be with Kizzy. I want to be with you, Isobel."

"That's a load of crap," Kieran says. "If you wanted her, you wouldn't have cheated on her. And with Kizzy Kane, of all people." He gestures in my direction. "You know what Verena did to Ryker's family."

I stand my ground, ready to defend Isobel. Now's not the time to rehash my past.

"I'm not getting into that," Garrett says. "All I'm saying is I'm done with Kizzy."

Isobel sniffles. "She's having your baby."

The strain in her words dredges up remnants of my own pain. The Kanes have wrecked so many lives, but their actions were a direct hit to Isobel and me.

I step back, allowing Kieran to take point, and squeeze Isobel's arm in reassurance.

Tears fall down her face. "How could I trust you again? How could I live as if everything is normal, knowing you have a child with another woman?"

Garrett throws his hand up. "How many times do I have to apologize until you forgive me?"

"You actually haven't apologized at all," I say.

"Well, I'm sorry. I messed up."

He's probably sick of Kizzy and wants to return to what he knows. Until the next woman comes along, and he throws it all away again.

Kieran points toward our dirt road. "Leave. We're done here."

Garrett scrubs his hands over his face. "Look, I'm not perfect, but I'll do better this time." His gaze drifts to Isobel. "What we had was good, right?"

"Don't answer that," Stephen says. "Remember what he's put you through."

Isobel straightens her back, her eyes narrowed on her ex-husband. "I want you to leave. And don't come back here."

Garrett sighs. "I'll leave, but I'm staying in town for a few days. Let me know if you want to talk."

He gets into his truck, and we stay where we are, all of us frozen like statues. Isobel holds it together until he drives away. She bursts into tears and drops her head into her hands.

Kieran wraps her in an embrace. "Don't let him get to you. You did good."

I clutch her shoulder. "We're here for you, Is."

"Don't worry," Stephen says. "We'll keep an eye out around town."

She pulls back from Kieran. "I just need some space."

We shadow her as she walks into the house. I don't know what to do, but we obviously can't leave her by herself.

She sighs. "Y'all don't have to babysit me. I'm a grown woman."

Kieran grabs her arm. "Isobel, it's okay to be hurt."

"This has affected all of us," I say. "We're in this together."

"It's mortifying," she says. "Everyone else noticed how Garrett acted, and I didn't. I was so naïve, and he took advantage of it. How could he treat me this way?" She hangs her head. "Didn't he love me at all?"

Stephen wraps an arm around her shoulders and leads her to the couch. Kieran glances at me, his eyes in slits, and I shake my head. I want to let the opinions fly, too. Fuel the fire burning inside me at the injustice served to our friend, and maybe lay a few punches into Garrett. But our concern is Isobel.

Stephen plops onto the cushions with her. She curls her feet onto the couch and leans into his side. I grab a blanket and drape it over her. Kieran sits on the couch by her feet and pats her legs.

And we all bear witness to her pain as she cries in Stephen's arms.

When she's calmer, she sits up and wipes her cheeks. "I'm sorry."

Kieran pats her legs again. "We've talked about this. Never be sorry for what Garrett did."

"We have work to do."

He grabs her hand and pulls her to her feet. "Not you. Get a nap in first."

She shakes her head. "It's too late in the day. Besides, I need to help."

"You'll help by resting." He jerks his head toward the stairs. "Just for a bit."

She walks away without arguing which is unusual for her. She trudges up the stairs and closes her door.

Kieran whirls on me. "If that son of a—"

I lift my hand. "I know. We all feel the same. But what Isobel needs is for us to stay calm."

He blows out a breath, spearing his fingers through his hair. "I need a minute." He spins around and marches down the hall. Though he's radiating fury, the front door closes softly.

Stephen drags his hand across the back of his neck. "Garrett has some nerve showing up here after what he did."

"I can't believe he thought Isobel would take him back."

He shakes his head as he walks toward the door. "We need to make sure she's never by herself."

"Agreed. He can't get her alone."

Garrett messed up when he hurt Isobel. If a man's involved with a woman, she's his top priority. If someone treated Sharona this way—

Sharona.

Shoot.

I lunge for my phone on the end table by the couch. An hour has passed since Sharona called me. And I have seventeen missed calls and twenty-eight unanswered texts from her, my mom, and Blake.

Instead of reading the multiple texts, I dial Sharona's number. For so many people to try to reach me, something must have happened. I should have answered her when she called me in the first place.

When I get her voicemail, I call my mom.

She picks up after the first ring. "Ryker Dane, why haven't you been answering your phone? Are you okay? Where are you? Did something happen?"

"Mom, Mom, Mom," I say, overlapping her many questions. "I'm fine. I'm okay."

"Then why didn't you answer your phone? Sharona's been trying to get ahold of you. Her mom's in the hospital."

The guilt inside me doubles. "Is her mom okay?"

"I'm not really sure."

"I'll apologize to her. Garrett showed up, so I stayed here with Isobel."

My mom pauses. "Garrett drove to the main house?"

I grab my coat and rush out the door. "Call Kieran and he'll tell you what happened. Did Sharona get to the hospital?"

"Yes, Blake gave her a ride. She went to Grapevine South Baptist."

"Then that's where I'm heading."

"I'm glad you're okay," she says, her voice softening.

I hop into my truck. "Thanks for checking, Mom."

"I love you."

"Love you, too."

When I hang up, I toss my phone onto the seat next to me and drive away from Fable Farms. I finally find a woman I want more than anything, and I keep messing up. I can only hope Sharona is blessed with patience.

CHAPTER 28

• • • ● • ● • ● • •

SHARONA

MY MOM LIES IN the ICU, beaten and unconscious. I stand by her bed, looking at the woman who I don't even know anymore.

I reach for her hand but stop and cross my arms instead. She might be in the hospital, but she's done too much damage.

Blake squeezes my shoulder. "You okay?"

"No." Bruises color my mother's skin. Bruises similar to the ones I've had before. "I'm conflicted."

"About?"

"Everything." I turn to him. "She's my mom, so I'm glad she's alright. But she didn't care about her kids. She let her boyfriends do whatever they wanted and never stood up for us. I shouldn't even care if she makes it."

Blake props his hands on the railing of my mom's hospital bed. "I get it. My ex-wife and I split because I didn't think she was the best mother. But I deal with her for my boys. They love her, and she still loves them."

"I used to think my mom loved me, but now I'm not sure."

He leaves my statement alone. I don't know if I want an answer. Do I want to know for certain if my mother doesn't love me?

"I can't believe Ryker's not here."

"Maybe something came up," Blake says. "I know he would want to be with you, if he could."

Someone knocks on the door. I turn around and see Ryker standing in the threshold.

The storm crashing inside me eases as I rush to him. He gathers me in his arms, and his presence settles a few more waves.

He squeezes my waist. "I'm sorry. I'm here now."

I pull back and rest my hands on his chest. "Are you okay? I tried calling and texting…"

"I'm okay. Nothing happened to me. Isobel's ex showed up, so I stayed to help her."

My brain circulates his words, analyzing them for meaning. Waves of nausea sweep through my stomach and disturb the sands of my sanity.

I step back, removing myself from his embrace. "You didn't pick me up because you were with Isobel?"

He was helping a friend.

But the thread of logic is no match for the storm of pain swelling once again within me.

Ryker frowns. "I was helping her."

My lip quivers. "You chose her over me."

"That's not what happened. I just… she needed me."

"*I* needed you! I wanted you with me, and you chose her."

He grabs my hand. "It's not like that. Isobel's been through a lot. She's family and…"

My heart shatters. I've clung to rule seven for so long, only trusting my brother. And I dared to hope I could trust Ryker. But I can't.

Because he doesn't want me.

"And I'm just someone you met a few weeks ago, so I don't come first."

He winces. "What? No. That's not what I mean."

"You say yes to everything and everyone. Except me."

"Sharona, that's not true."

"You don't consider me important."

"You're one of the most important people in my life."

Tears flow down my cheeks. "Unfortunately, your words don't mean much to me anymore. I wish they did."

Every time I've needed him, he's chosen someone else. I was willing to want him, to choose him, to fall in love, but he doesn't feel the same.

My rules straighten their bent edges, and the ones I broke mend themselves in my mind. Like walls of a castle, my rules protect me. Saint gave them to me for a reason.

No more opening myself up to new people. No more searching for some sort of belonging. No more looking for love.

Rule One: Don't fall in love.

That rule was at the top of my list. The most important, and now the one that will last to the end. Because the man I would have broken it for stands within my reach, but he doesn't choose me.

I shuffle away from Ryker, creating more space between us. "I want you to leave."

"Sharona, hold on a second."

"I need you to leave."

"Can I just talk to you?"

"No, stay away from me."

Blake slides close to my side.

I shake my head. "You've been playing the good guy, trying to win my trust, but you don't care."

"How can you say that?" Ryker asks.

"Because you don't." A harsh laugh leaves me. "I should've known better. You're just like all of them."

"Who?"

"Men who think they can fling a woman aside and then wash away their actions with pretty words."

His hands ball into fists. "You know I'm not like that. I treat everyone with respect, especially you."

"I deserve someone who chooses me."

"You're the one who got upset when you thought I was choosing you over Stephen. Now there's a time when someone else needs me, and you get angry with me? How is that fair?"

"It's not the same. I just want you to choose me at least once."

"And I have. But I have lots of people who count on me."

His words knock me down. "I need space to think."

Blake wraps his arm around my shoulders. "I think you should go, Ryker. I'll text you later."

Ryker pinches the bridge of his nose. He drops his hand and meets my gaze. "Please let me stay."

But I can't let him. It's time we end this for good.

So I say the last word I ever thought I'd say to the man in front of me. "Leave."

CHAPTER 29

· · · · ● · ● · ● · · ·

SHARONA

I STAYED AT THE hospital overnight. With everything my mom has done, I shouldn't have. But I couldn't find it in myself to leave.

She woke up early this morning. After the doctor decided she was stable, they moved her out of ICU late afternoon. I didn't talk to her much, but I was here for her. More than what she ever did for me.

My phone vibrates with a text.

Blake:

> Got stuck in traffic. Be there in fifteen.

I've been texting him and Genevieve all day with updates on my mom. When I told them I wasn't going back to Fable Farms, Genevieve drove to the hospital to see what was going on with me. I told her about my fight with Ryker, and she convinced me to stay at her brother's house tonight.

The heart rate monitor beeps to the left of my chair as my mom rests in the hospital bed in her new room. I wrap both of my hands around a paper cup of coffee. It's after six in the evening, so I won't chance the caffeine. But I crave the warmth.

For my hands.

For my soul.

My mother stirs, and her eyes flutter open. "Sharona? What are you still doing here?"

I place my cup on the table next to me. "I'm here in case you need anything."

"Can I sit up?"

Guess I'm not going to get a thank you for staying here all night.

I lift the bed to an inclined position, so she can still rest.

She grabs my hand. "I'm glad to see you. I've been worried about you."

"Have you?"

"Of course."

My pulse jumps as adrenaline pours into my veins. First Ryker and now my mom. Why do people say they care about me when they don't show it?

I clench my teeth to keep the words I shouldn't say inside me.

"You can't leave like you did," she says. "We need each other."

The muscles in my neck strain as I bottle everything up.

She squeezes my hand. "You're the only one I have since Saint's gone."

The cork flies off the bottle, and my emotions spill over. "Yeah, because you killed him."

"What? Why would you say that to me?"

"Because it's true!" I fling her hand away from me and jump to my feet. "He died from too many drugs. Drugs he wouldn't have had his hands on if it wasn't for you. Because he was keeping me out of the house and away from your boyfriend at the time."

Her whole face scrunches. "I've been trying to provide for us."

"Saint provided for me. While you were using and getting drunk and who knows what else, he was the one person I could count on."

When tears spring up, I let them fall. I unleash my pain and let it flow over me.

Let it hurt.

Let it overwhelm me so I can grieve the one person who cared more about me than himself.

Mom frowns. "You can count on me."

"Yeah, like I could count on you to protect me from all the boyfriends you brought around the house?"

"I didn't know—"

"No, you don't get to play the pity card. After everything I've been through, you deserve to feel guilty. You deserve to feel loss and anguish. You are the cause of all my problems, and you don't get to look the other way anymore!"

She gasps. "You can't talk to me this way. I'm your mother."

"Please. You haven't acted like a true mother in years."

"I've put a roof over your head, food in the kitchen, gave you a bed and an education. What more do you want?"

"Someone who actually cares about me! Who spends time with me and takes care of me." Tears stream down my cheeks. "Someone who watches out for me. Someone who puts me first."

"I care about you. You're my daughter. I love you."

I shake my head. "I'm not even sure you know what love is."

She looks away and shuffles down into the bed. "I think you should leave. I need to rest."

"I'm the only one who's been here for you, and you don't even care."

She waves her hand toward the door. "Leave. Go. I don't want you here."

"What's new, Mom?"

I storm out and head to the waiting room. My tears continue as I find a chair away from all the other visitors. I wrap my arms around myself, my mom's words cycling through my mind.

I don't want you here.

How did this spiral so far out of control? What happened to the mother who tucked me into bed? Who let Saint and me pick whatever movie we wanted to see at the theater? Who gave us a good life before she stripped it all away?

I don't want you here.

Ryker's face pops into my mind, and I glare at the tile floor. He fed me small acts of kindness until that was all I craved. Then he shoved me aside like I was nothing.

I don't want you here.

Saint should be here with me. I'll never know why he had those drugs at the party. If he had left them alone, followed rule two, he would still be here. But he's gone. He left me.

Everyone I thought I could trust disappointed me.

I have no one.

Gwen was wrong. Some people can't be forgiven. I just have to accept that my mother doesn't see how she took away all the good in my life and gave me only bad.

Blake steps into the waiting room with a frown. He walks my way and sits in the chair next to me. "I tried texting you that I was here, and you didn't answer. What's wrong?"

One sob bubbles up followed by another. My crying grows desperate, and I drop my head into my hands.

Blake pats my back.

I lift my head and glare at him. "I'm angry."

"It's okay to be angry. We're only human."

"Nobody cares. My mom ruined my life. She's the reason my brother's dead, and the reason I ran away to begin with. Ryker made me think he cares, but he let me down, too. And Saint left me. He never did drugs, and the one time he did, changed my life completely. What is wrong with everyone?"

Blake's eyes soften. "Nothing's wrong. People hurt you, and it's hard when they're people you love and trust. But you find the strength to forgive them."

"That's what Gwen said, but I can't forgive them."

"I didn't think I could forgive my ex-wife for what she did to me, but I eventually moved past it."

"How?"

He shrugs. "I just didn't want to waste any more time thinking about her, good or bad. Instead, I spent my time with the people I love."

"I don't have anybody."

"You haven't had an easy life, Sharona. But I hope you know you can count on me."

"That's what everyone says. And then they disappoint me."

He sighs. "Like I said, we're only human. People will disappoint you, and you'll disappoint people. Nobody's perfect. But the times people are there for you make up for the times they're not."

"None of them have been there for me when I need it."

"Is there a good memory of your mom that you can think of?"

An image flashes in my mind of my mom snuggling me on the couch when I was about eight. I stayed home because I was sick, and she helped me have the best day.

"Maybe."

Blake clasps his hands together. "And your brother might have made a bad choice the night he died, but what about all the good he did? I've heard you talk about him. You loved him a lot."

I sniffle. "Yes. I did."

"And Ryker? He's a good man, and I know he's done a lot for you."

I think back on my first day at Fable Farms. Ryker tried so hard to prove to me that I didn't have to be scared of him. I was a stranger, yet he showed me kindness.

My mind fills with snapshots of these past few weeks.

Ryker protecting me from the steer.

His smile when he talked about his family.

The steady gaze of his blue eyes as he gave me his jacket at the festival.

His protection and comfort when I freaked out in the diner.

But I'm confused. Do the small instances where he was there for me outweigh the bigger mistakes he's made? It doesn't feel like they do.

I wipe my cheeks. "Can we leave now?"

Blake nods. "Sure. Just think about what I said, okay?"

We walk to his truck in silence, and I do think about what he said. During the drive back to his place, I think. When I'm lying on the air mattress in his living room, I think.

But at the end of the night, all my thoughts only bring me more hurt and uncertainty.

CHAPTER 30

· · · · ● · ● · · ·

SHARONA

BLAKE PULLS UP TO the hospital the next morning and parks his truck. "You want me to go with you?"

I stare at the sliding doors. "No, I'll be fine."

This might be a terrible idea. After our fight yesterday, I doubt my mom will want to see me. Discussing the past won't fix the broken years of my life.

But a good daughter would visit her mother in the hospital. And although Marilyn Bennett hasn't been a good mother in years, I'm a good daughter.

I get out of the truck. "Thanks for dropping me off."

"I'll be back around supper time," Blake says. "Unless I hear differently from you."

"Do you think you could get my things from the main house?"

Since my fight with Ryker two nights ago, I've been staying at Blake's. Genevieve has let me borrow clothes and toiletries, but it's time I take my stuff out of the main house. I don't see myself going back to Fable Farms anytime soon.

Blake frowns. "Sure. If that's what you want, I can do that."

I busy myself with my purse. "It's what I want."

When I enter the hospital, the lull in the waiting room adds to my indifference. My sneakers squeak against the white tiles as I walk down the cold corridor. I reach my mom's room and open the door.

Her gaze snaps toward me. "Are you here to apologize?"

Heat flows through my veins, and I try to focus on Blake's words.

The times people are there for you make up for the times they're not.

I take a seat in the chair next to her bed. "Did you sleep well?"

"Are you not sorry?"

"Are you?"

"I expect an apology for what you said yesterday. It was very disrespectful."

"Because you've respected me? Because the way you've treated me has been golden?"

"If you just came to argue, then you can leave."

"What happened to you? Do you not love me at all? What about Saint? What did we do to make you treat us this way?"

Her eyes shift to the window.

My pulse spikes at her ignoring me. I take a deep breath, ready to fight. For myself and for Saint.

"I never wanted this," she says.

I blink, the adrenaline frozen in my veins.

She twists her hands in her lap. "We were happy... the three of us. And I ruined it."

Good. She's not denying it. She should feel bad for once in her life.

Her lips tremble. "I loved being a mother, but it just got hard. I had no one to help me."

So? I had nobody, and I found a way to survive. A way to keep my values.

When she looks back at me, a tear trails down her face. "I can't believe what I've done to you. I've hurt you. My beautiful daughter."

My jaw drops.

She grabs my hand, and I can't find it in myself to pull away.

"You had to be strong," she says. "You and Saint kept it all together when I didn't." Her face crumbles. "And my baby boy died… because of me." She drops her head into her hands and sobs.

This is what I've waited for. For her to admit she's wrong, to admit she's been a terrible mother.

But the satisfaction I've wanted for so long is missing.

My mother lies in a hospital bed as I shove more agony her way, wanting her to suffer. If I hold my pain against her, intentionally try to hurt her, I would be a cruel person. And that's not me.

The blame I've thrown her way fades like the setting sun.

When I left her on my birthday, I was broken. My big brother had died, my mother was drinking her life away, and men had poisoned my view on relationships.

But since I've been at Fable Farms, with the community of Mustang Cross, I've gained new memories. Started replacing the bad with good. I've found a home and stepped into a stronger version of myself.

I swallow hard. "It's okay."

She grips my hand. "I'm sorry. I'm so sorry."

A record of what she's done rolls through my mind and mixes with memories of who she used to be. Who *we* used to be. The pieces of our life fit like stained glass, each with jagged edges but creating an image with potential. And thoughts of who we could be, if I gave her a chance, add to the mosaic of my relationship with my mother.

"Maybe… we can start over."

She wipes a tear. "And you came to help me. After everything I did."

I fidget with her blanket. "You're my mom."

"I've missed you."

My shoulders drop. "I've missed you, too."

"You look different."

"I am different."

"More peaceful."

My mind fills with the faces of the people I've met these past few weeks. "I've been living with some people from Mustang Cross. It's a great place."

"Why don't you tell me about it? I want to know what you've been up to."

"You should rest first."

She situates her pillow. "I am a bit tired."

"Get some sleep. Then we can talk." I chew on my lip. "Do you... do you want to sing our song?"

When Saint and I were little—when it was the three of us and we were happy—my mom would sing us a lullaby at night. She would soothe us to sleep, and it would be the perfect ending to our day. Though she hasn't sung the song in years, I remember every word.

Her eyes soften. "I would love that."

I scoot the chair closer to the bed and grab her hand.

And we sing our song.

Why don't you come, come with me?

Maybe to the river, river or the road

Maybe to the meadow, meadow or the tree

Anywhere, anywhere I'll go

Just know, know that I'm there

Even if you're glad, glad or blue

Even if you're weak, weak or scared

I'm always, always with you

A smile spreads across her face as we sing the song again. I rest my head on the bed and close my eyes. She releases my hand and slides her fingers through my long hair.

And I allow her to comfort me and be what I've always wanted.

A mother.

CHAPTER 31

• • • • • • • • • • •

RYKER

ON SATURDAY MORNING, I do something I never do.

I take the day off.

Before the sun rises, I text the group that I need a few hours to myself. After two restless nights, a change of pace might help me clear my mind.

I drive to my spot and sit on the tailgate. The fields stretch in front of me as I take in Fable Farms. What was once my center and my foundation.

But the sight of my family's legacy brings me little peace today.

My chest feels like a rock. No, a cave. Dark, cold, and hollow.

In a matter of weeks, Sharona took pieces of my heart until I had no choice but to surrender it all. Carve it out of my chest and hand it to her.

I've never loved a woman the way I love her.

My mind flashes to our fight at the hospital. I scrub my hands over my face. She stared at me like she needed to cling to something, and I was the thinnest branch on the tree.

The woman I love thought she wasn't important, and I couldn't even get close to her to convince her otherwise.

After I spend a few hours at my spot, I head back to the main house. As I walk onto the porch, I figure I need to help with lunch.

I stop in my tracks.

I'm still doing it. I can't stop putting others first even when I need a break.

I stomp into the house, toe off my boots, and plop down onto the couch.

Helping people is second nature. But I've let it take over my life. I've given up what I want, what I need, to help others. And I've damaged my relationship with Sharona because of it.

Isobel sits next to me and places a mug in my hands. "How're you doing?"

She, Kieran, and Stephen bombarded me yesterday morning. Everyone was coming off Garrett's sudden reappearance Thursday, so I didn't want to give them more to worry about. But all of them are tenacious in their own way.

I finally told them about my argument with Sharona and about what happened to her mom. I just haven't divulged all my thoughts and how I'm second-guessing everything I am.

I fiddle with the mug in my hands. "How do you think?"

Kieran sits in the armchair, and it creaks under his weight.

Isobel nudges my knee. "I wouldn't put too much weight into what Sharona said. She'll be back. She likes you."

"She doesn't think she's important to me," I say. "She thinks I put everyone else above her."

Isobel frowns. "That's ridiculous. Why would she think you put others first?"

"Because I forgot to pick her up on Thanksgiving, and when Garrett showed up, I chose to stay here instead of taking her call. If I had, I would have known about her mom sooner."

Sharona was partially right. The times she's needed me, I've pushed her aside in favor of my friends. But how do I find a balance? She got upset when she thought she was coming between my friends and me, but also when I didn't choose her. How am I supposed to help everyone if they all need me at once?

Kieran's brows furrow. "I never thought about it like that."

"Neither have I," Isobel says. "You're just so dependable. Kieran's the grump, Stephen's the comedian, I'm the intelligent one—"

"Watch it," Kieran says.

"—and you're the sweet one. You're always there if we need you."

I swirl the coffee in my mug. "And I don't mind."

"We know. But perhaps we rely on you too much." She stands and takes my mug, I guess knowing I won't drink the coffee. "It's okay for you to say no sometimes. We'll understand."

She walks away, and Kieran follows her without a word.

I lean my head back on the couch. Helping others has been a poor substitute for a family of my own, and my priorities need to shift. I have to find a way to fix this mess, to find a balance and show Sharona we can make it work.

To prove to her she's all I want.

The front door opens, but I keep staring at the ceiling.

"Hey, Ryker," Blake says.

"Hey. I'll get started on lunch in a bit."

"Why don't y'all go out and help Isobel and Kieran?" Blake says. "I need a minute with Ryker."

Whoever he's talking to walks away, and the door shuts again.

Blake circles the couch and sits next to me. "Don't remember the last time you asked for a day off."

"I'm not feeling the greatest today."

"Want to talk about it?"

"I spoke with Kieran and Isobel. I'm fine."

He scratches his jaw. "Sharona wants me to pack up her things."

His words tumble onto me like a pile of bricks. "Sounds like she's running again."

"I'll keep an eye on her. I spoke with her last night. She's hit a rough patch with her mom and going through some things. I dropped her off at the hospital this morning, but she didn't seem excited to be there."

Sharona confided in Blake and not me.

That burns like bull nettle.

She should tell me things, turn to me, rely on me. But I've messed up too many times.

I hang my head and run my fingers through my hair. "She's never gonna let me near her."

"She still cares about you," Blake says.

"She wants nothing to do with me."

"She's taking it as hard as you are. That says something."

"Don't know why she'd be upset. She's the one who wanted space."

"Sometimes we don't make the best decisions when we're hurting."

I clasp my hands together. "I hate to put you in this situation... but could you do me a favor? Could you ask her if I can come see her at the hospital?"

"Sure. Don't think anything of it."

"Thanks. I appreciate it."

He blows out a breath and stands. "I better get her things. Why don't I help you with lunch when I'm done."

I get to my feet. "Sure. I'll be in the kitchen."

"Just be patient. Sharona's been through a lot, but she'll come around."

As he walks away, I think about what I can do to bring Sharona around faster. She needs to know I value her and will put her first.

I haven't been worried about what I want in so long, but what I want is to settle down and start a family.

What I want is Sharona.

The next time I see her, my mission is to make sure she knows I love her.

CHAPTER 32

• • • • ● • ● • • •

SHARONA

FOR THE FIRST TIME in years, I have a smile on my face as I talk with my mother. She eats dinner in her hospital room while I tell her about my stay in Mustang Cross.

Our conversation this morning feels like a stepping stone. We may have to take a few more steps to fix our relationship, but we're headed down the right path.

Her eyes widen. "And the cows were close enough for you to touch? Right in front of you?"

I laugh. "Yes. It was so much fun."

A knock sounds at the door, and I turn to see Blake saunter into the room.

He removes his cowboy hat. "Good evening, Sharona. Ms. Bennett. You're looking better."

My mom's nose scrunches. "Just don't call me Ms. Bennett again. That makes me sound ancient."

I snort as she extends her hand to Blake.

"Sharona tells me you were here the day I was admitted," she says.

I gesture to the blond man next to me. "Mom, this is Blake. Remember, his sister's Genevieve? The woman I've been telling you about?"

"Ah, yes. Nice to meet you."

Blake releases her hand. "Nice to meet you, too, uh..."

"Marilyn. Call me Marilyn."

He nods and looks at me. "Can I speak with you in private?"

"You can talk to me here. My mom can hear what you have to say."

She waves her hand toward me. "I'm fine, Shar. Go talk with him."

"I don't have any secrets. Just tell me."

Blake blows out a breath. "Ryker wanted to know if he could visit."

Heat travels up my neck and burns my face like the rays of the sun.

So I have one secret.

In my conversations with my mom, I left out the guy who smashed through my defenses. I didn't know if I could handle her asking for details about him.

"Tell him no," I say to Blake.

"He really wants to be here," he says. "With you."

"Blake, stop. I don't want to talk to him or see him right now."

He sighs. "Okay, fine. It's your choice. You ready to go?"

"Would you mind giving us a minute, Blake?" Mom asks. "We won't be long."

I should have known she wouldn't ignore this.

Blake pats my shoulder. "Sure. Whenever you're ready, I'll be in the waiting room."

As soon as he leaves the room, my mom latches onto my hand.

"What was that about?" she asks.

"Nothing."

"Who's Ryker?"

The heat from earlier doubles, blasting against my face. "Nobody."

She giggles like a giddy teenage girl. "Is he your boyfriend?"

"What? No. It's not... I don't know."

"Have you two kissed yet?"

I duck my head.

She lets loose a cackle. "You have. Why isn't he here with you?"

"He was here the day you came to the hospital, but I told him to leave."

"Why would you do that?"

"Because I didn't want to see him."

She frowns.

I pull my hand away from hers and pick at the corner of her blanket. "He let me down. I can't trust him, or any man for that matter. They're all the same."

"What on earth are you talking about?"

"Mom, please. I've been around men my whole life, and they take what they want and end up hurting women."

The pucker in her brows deepens. "This is my fault."

I shake my head. "I've realized there's no man I can trust. Not like Saint."

"What about Blake?"

I stiffen. "It's different."

"Tell me something. You spoke about all these men at Fable Farms. What do you think of them?"

They're good.

Her eyes soften. "Not all men are bad. Do you trust Blake?"

"Yes."

"Because he hasn't let you down yet. But he will. Everyone will let you down."

"Ryker wasn't there when I needed him."

"Sounds like he wants a second chance."

"Maybe."

"Then give him another chance. A chance to choose you."

"What if he doesn't?"

"It'll hurt, but you'll move on." She glances at her lap. "I know it might seem like men are replaceable because of how I've lived, but if you find the right one, the right kind of love, it will feel anything but replaceable." The smile she gives me is strained. "I've been trying to find it my whole life. You're lucky you found it so young."

Love? Do I love Ryker?

Images float through my mind and blend into a picture of my relationship with him. He's helpful, kind, and gentle with me. He protects me and kisses like a dream.

I do love him.

I shouldn't have pushed him away. His helpful spirit is one of the things I love about him. I should be proud he helps so many.

Do I want him to be there for me? Yes. But I need to understand he has others who need him. Because who wouldn't need him? He's the best man I know.

I reach for my mom's hand. "You could still find it."

She shrugs. "Maybe."

I stand and grab my purse. "I'll come back tomorrow."

"Wait!" She reaches toward the side table and grabs her car keys. "I almost forgot. Can you do me a favor?"

"Sure."

She winces. "My car must still be at Perky's Bar. Would you be able to move it? I'd hate for it to get towed."

I take the keys from her outstretched hand. "How am I supposed to move it without a license?"

"Oh, honey, not you. Maybe you can ask Blake or another friend of yours. I can't afford for it to get towed."

Her gaze flicks to the door before returning to me. She beckons me closer, and I step to the edge of her bed.

"We'll be fine, Sharona," she says, dropping her voice to a whisper. "I can get us some money. Jimmy's stashed a couple thousand in our closet back at the house."

"Mom, you can't go back there."

"It'll be fine. I'll go when Jimmy isn't home. I know exactly where it is. But if you can move my car, that would help. Can't get any fines."

"No, yeah. I'll handle it." I kiss her cheek. "Get some rest. I'll see you tomorrow."

When I meet Blake in the waiting room, we walk out to his truck. Evening creeps closer and transforms the sky with streaks of purple, orange, and pink.

My mom's words flow like a river through my mind.

Her car. The house. Hidden money.

An idea sparks like flint against rock, and my fingers curl around her car keys. If my mom returns to that house, Jimmy won't think twice about hurting her again. She'll be in the same danger, or she might not even escape this time.

But I can help her.

I'm the only one who can.

CHAPTER 33

· · · ·•· ●· ●· · ·

SHARONA

GENEVIEVE DROPS ME OFF at the hospital the next afternoon around lunch. As soon as I'm hidden inside the building, I call a rideshare. My stomach knots for lying to Genevieve, but nobody can know about my plan. Not even one of my closest friends.

The driver takes me to Perky's Bar to pick up my mom's beat-up sedan. Fortunately, the driver takes my cash when she drops me off. The knots in my stomach tighten as my cash fund dwindles, but I focus on the money I hope to find soon.

Raindrops fall on the windshield as I drive through the rural neighborhood. The wipers clear my view, and I slow the car to a crawl. I park in front of the house my mom has been sharing with Jimmy. His truck is missing from the driveway. That's a good sign.

My fingers unclench the steering wheel. Every part of me was tense during my drive. I felt like a neon sign was pointed at me—a signal to all the cops that I was driving without a license.

I grab my phone and scroll through my contacts. The names of the friends I've made in Mustang Cross appear in my list.

Maybe this is wrong. Maybe I should tell someone where I am. Jimmy could show up at any time. At the very least, I could text Genevieve my address. Just in case.

I drop my phone onto the seat next to me and turn off the car. I can do this myself. I'll go in really quick, grab the cash, and leave. A few minutes, and I'll have more money. One of my problems will be solved.

After another look at the empty street, I slide out of the car. The drizzle seeps into my hair and clothes, chilling my skin. I pull on Saint's jacket. It offers me little protection from the weather, but I couldn't face this house again without feeling my brother close to me.

Once I reach back in for my mom's keys and my phone, I slam the car door and jog to the house. The overhang above the door blocks me from the rain. My hands fumble with my mom's key ring until I find the house key. I unlock the door and hurry inside.

Silence hangs throughout the house. My pulse jumps.

Get in and get out. Halfway there.

When I enter my mom's bedroom, I cringe in the midst of Jimmy's living space. Clothes litter the carpet, and an assortment of drugs spreads out on top of the desk against the wall. I rush to the closet and begin my search.

I toss aside a few pairs of shoes, look through the boxes on the floor, and come up empty. I yank the clothes hanging on the rack to clear my way to the back of the closet. As I part two of my mom's blouses, I find a shoebox resting on a shelf. I pull it out and crack the lid open.

My stomach twists at the sight of the bills stashed inside. I'm almost positive this money was earned illegally. Or at least in the gray area. But we need it. This is the best option for my mom and me.

The front door slams. I clutch the shoebox and spin toward the bedroom's threshold.

"Marilyn?"

My heart skitters at Jimmy's rough voice. I lunge toward the bed and drop to my knees. My belly scrapes against the carpet as I slide underneath the bed. I settle the box next to me and grip it tight.

"Marilyn!" Jimmy's voice booms. "I saw your car, you ungrateful, little—"

He calls my mom an awful name, and I wince. I reach into my pocket for my phone. My reservations fly out the window, and I scroll to the number of the only person I want near me.

I press the phone to my ear, praying he answers. And God must hear me.

"Sharona?" Ryker says.

Tears form at the wonderful voice I haven't heard in days. "Ryker?"

He sighs. "Sharona. It's good to hear from you."

"I need help."

"Marilyn!" Jimmy shouts again, his voice sounding further away. He must be searching the house.

He'll come to the bedroom soon.

"What's going on?" Ryker asks. His voice hardens, so unlike the soothing man I know.

"I'm at my mom's house, and her boyfriend is here."

He pauses. "Wait... what are you doing there?"

"I was trying to get some money—it doesn't matter. I'm here, and I don't know what to do."

Jimmy calls my mom's name again.

I lower my voice to a breath of a whisper. "He's walking through the house."

"Get out of there," Ryker says. "Now."

"I don't know if I can make it to the door without being seen."

"Can you hide somewhere?"

"I'm under the bed."

"Stay there and stay quiet. Send me the address."

My fingers shake as I text him my mom's address. "I just did."

"Marilyn?"

I flinch at the singsong turn of Jimmy's voice. He's closer to the room.

"Ryker"—Gwen's voice comes through the line—"who are you talking to?"

My forehead digs into the carpet. Sunday lunch with his family. The most important people in his life. I can't bear another rejection.

"You're busy. Forget I asked."

"I'm not busy," Ryker says. "I promise I'm coming for you."

Even though a part of me still wants to believe him, my hope has been dashed to pieces. He won't show up. Or at least, won't show up until it's too late.

I hang up and turn my phone off, so I don't attract Jimmy's attention. My eyes lock on the bedroom door as I stick my phone back in my pocket.

Footsteps sound in the hall, growing closer. I clamp my hand over my mouth to stifle my breathing.

A pair of boots appears in the open doorway, and my fingers clench the shoebox full of cash.

Jimmy saunters into the room and heads to the closet. He rummages around, curses, and tosses something hard against the wall. I wince as tears stream down my face.

And as fast as the tears arrive, a prayer floats on their coat-tails—a prayer to keep me safe. The people at Fable Farms pray like they need it to survive. Like it brings them everything good.

I could use a little good right now.

Jimmy walks around the bed, and I stay as still as I can. Rustling and other sounds fill the room, but I have no clue what he's doing.

My body trembles. I press my hand harder against my mouth, worried that Jimmy can hear my breathing. The metallic tang of blood hits my tongue as my teeth cut into my lips.

His boots move around the room and stop on the side of the bed.

My breath hitches. A soft rustling sounds from above.

Jimmy kneels next to the bed.

He places his hands on the floor.

And looks directly at me.

CHAPTER 34

· · · · ● · ● · ● · ·

SHARONA

I CRY OUT AND jerk back, hitting my head on the bedframe.

Jimmy seizes my arm and pulls me toward him. "Look who I found. A little thief trying to steal from me."

I claw at the carpet, searching for traction, and lose my hold on the shoebox.

My only reason for being here in the first place.

He drags me out from beneath the bed and tugs me to my feet. I push against him and flail my arms like a drowning swimmer. When he grips me by both arms, I'm grateful for the extra padding from Saint's jacket.

Jimmy grabs my chin, his grip bruising. "You take from me, Sharona, I take from you."

I struggle against him. "Please, I'm sorry. I won't take the money."

"Too late," he says. "Seems like what I've wanted for a while is now your price for stealing."

A knock on the front door reaches my ears. Though it might be naïve, my whole being reaches out as if Ryker has come to save me.

I break from Jimmy's hold and scream toward the open bedroom door.

Jimmy clamps his hand over my mouth. "Quiet."

I strain against his grasp, yelling into his palm.

"Sharona?"

When Ryker shouts my name, tears spark in my eyes.

Jimmy lets loose a stream of obscene words. He tugs me toward the closet, and his hand slips off my mouth.

I seize the chance and raise my voice. "Ryker!"

"Sharona!" Ryker yells, louder than before.

Hope buoys me even as Jimmy pins my back to his front and once again plasters his hand over my mouth.

And as the revolting man behind me faces the door, using me as a shield, the gentlest man I've ever known rushes into the bedroom.

Ryker came.

He chose me.

The man I've pushed away for days came to save me.

And he brought everyone.

Ryker's eyes zero in on where I'm standing with Jimmy. The others from Fable Farms crowd into the room. Kieran and Isobel flank Ryker. Stephen stands behind them, and Blake's at his side with a revolver in his hand.

My tears multiply at the sight of my friends—my *family*—who came to rescue me.

Jimmy steps back, still holding me in front of him. "Leave, or I'll call the cops. You're trespassing."

Kieran's eyes narrow. "And you're assaulting. I wonder which offense the cops will treat more seriously."

Jimmy pushes me away from him. "She was stealing from me. I have a right to protect my property." He points his finger at the Fable Farms crew. "Including pressing charges for breaking and entering."

Stephen shrugs. "The door was open, but go ahead. Call the cops. I'm sure they won't ask to search the house or notice the possession of illegal drugs."

Ryker beckons me toward him. "Come here, Sharona."

Everything from the past few days washes away. All I want is to feel his arms around me. Feel his lips on mine. Listen to his soothing voice.

And I run to him.

I throw my arms around his neck as he wraps his own around my waist. I close my eyes, relishing the safety of his embrace.

His hold on me tightens. "I got you, baby. You're okay." He exhales a breath into my neck. "I've missed you so much."

"You came."

"Of course. I told you I would, and I plan to keep my promises to you from here on out."

"You plan on making more promises to me?"

"As many as you'll take." He pulls away and cradles my face in his hands. "Did he hit you? Are you hurt?"

I grab onto his wrists. "I'm fine. I just want to leave. Please."

He glances behind me. "Don't contact Sharona or her mother, and don't come anywhere near them."

Jimmy swears at him, throwing out words I've never heard but must be bad.

"You think I can punch him and get away with it?" Kieran asks.

"He's not worth it," Isobel says.

Jimmy blusters, and the others handle the situation. But I focus on Ryker. My home.

He hoists me into his arms, and I wrap my legs around his waist.

"Let's get you out of here," he says.

He carries me through the house, and I prop my chin on his shoulder. The rain falls harder as he walks outside. I burrow deeper against him, trusting him to take care of me.

After he's walked a few steps, he stops and kisses my jaw. "Let me get you into my truck, baby."

I unwind myself from him and jump to the ground. Ready to get away from this house. Ready to go home.

Kieran steps next to him. "Give me the keys. I'll drive."

Ryker hands him the keys as I climb into the passenger seat. He crawls into the truck behind me, forcing me into the middle. He helps me out of Saint's jacket and tosses it onto his back seat. When he's fastening my seatbelt for me, I notice how shaky his hands are.

I place my hand on his. "I'm okay."

His gaze locks on mine. "You have no idea how scared I was. Thinking I wouldn't get to you in time."

He shakes his head and loosens my seatbelt before buckling his. When he tugs me toward him and wraps his arm around me, I realize why he needed my seatbelt a little loose.

So I could be close to him.

His arm tightens around me. "The image of that guy with his hands on you is burned in my mind. I just need a moment."

I lay my head on his chest and drape my arm across his stomach.

A breath stutters out of him. "You're okay."

I squeeze his waist. "I'm okay."

His knuckles slide up and down my arm, soothing me. I must doze off because I'm groggy when he carries me out of the truck. I lift my head, but he lowers his mouth to my ear.

"Just sleep, baby. I got you."

We move from the truck to someplace soft. Everything feels slow yet fast. Sluggish yet too quick. When Ryker shifts back, my eyes fly open. I can't let him leave me now that I have him.

He removes his arms from around me, and I grip the front of his shirt.

"Wait, don't go."

He runs his hand over my head. "I'm right here."

"Don't leave."

"Can one of you get a blanket?" he asks, his voice a whisper.

He encourages me to lie down, and I welcome sleep.

CHAPTER 35

• • • • • • • • • • •

SHARONA

THIS IS THE BEST bed I've ever slept in. Did my bed at Fable Farms feel this comfortable? Am I in a fancy hotel?

"You still doing okay?"

Is someone here?

"Yeah, I'm good."

"Let us know if you need anything."

The bed drags my focus back to it, its warmth and softness wrapping around me.

My brows scrunch together. Beds don't wrap around people.

I open my eyes and stare at a chest.

A man's chest.

I'm completely wrapped around him. Arms and legs, the whole shebang. Like a koala.

What. Is. Happening.

I yelp and try to scramble out of the arms holding me.

"Shh, calm down." The man's voice draws my focus to his face.

Ryker.

My body relaxes. "Sorry."

He runs his hand down my hair. "You're fine. Did you sleep well?"

"Yes, but what are you doing in my room?"

"We're on the couch," he says.

"Oh. What are we doing here?"

"You were out of it, so I just let you sleep on the couch. Better for everyone to keep an eye on you."

"Everyone's been watching over me?"

"Yeah, to make sure you're okay."

"And you're cuddling with me because..."

He tugs me closer like he can't get enough of touching me. "You asked me to."

The blood rushes to my cheeks. "What? I asked you to cuddle with me?"

"Not cuddle. You asked me to stay with you. This seemed like the easiest option."

"How long have I been asleep?"

"About five hours. It's six now."

"You must have to pee so bad." I clap my hand over my mouth. "Morning breath. Or I guess sleep breath since it's not technically morning."

He laughs and nuzzles his face into my neck. "I love you."

I suck in a breath. Did he say love?

He pulls back with a sigh. "Sorry, that just slipped out."

My body stiffens. So he doesn't love me? He's taking it back?

"No, it's fine. It's okay if you didn't mean it."

"Of course, I mean it. I just didn't want to freak you out." He cups my cheek. "Sharona, I'm in love with you."

I drop my head to hide my face. "Stop. Please."

"I know it's only been about a month, so I don't want you to feel any pressure."

"How can I not feel pressure with that?"

He tilts my chin until I meet his gaze. "Baby, you don't have to say it back. I understand it might take longer for you to get there."

"What if I never get there?"

His brows slant down. "Then I'll deal with it. But you'll always be the one for me."

Tears form in my eyes. "What if I'm not good enough for you?"

"Don't say that. You're perfect for me."

Perfect for him? He's the one who's perfect. He's the golden boy of Mustang Cross who can do no wrong.

And he wants me.

He releases a deep sigh. "Feels so good having you in my arms."

It does feel good. It feels right, us together. Nothing has felt more right than being with him.

"I'm sorry for what I did," I say. "For pushing you away. For running."

"It's not all your fault. I messed up, too. I should have been there for you."

"I should have trusted you. I know you help a lot of people, and I'm going to try to be more understanding."

"We're both learning."

"I can't believe you missed your family lunch to come get me."

He kisses my cheek. "I'm learning I need to say no to some things."

"But they're your family."

"You're my family, too," he says. "And I didn't say no to them forever, just one meal. Finding you was more important."

I chew on my lip. "Thank you. For saving me."

"I'd do it again. Anything for you."

And I'd do anything for him. He's the only man I'll ever want. He knows when to respect my boundaries but also when to knock them down so I can truly live my life.

That's what Ryker does. He helps me live. And he helps me love.

I'm in love with him, and I shouldn't be scared to tell him.

I tilt my head down and inhale the scent of home. "I love you."

Ryker stiffens and pulls back. "You don't have to say it because I did. I want you to mean it if you say it."

"I do mean it. I love you."

He cups my jaw. "Really?"

I nestle into his palm. "Yes. And I can't believe we're having this conversation on the couch."

He tucks my head against his chest. "Best moment of my life."

I'm glad he can't see my face, because I'm worried the big smile on my face makes me look like a goofball.

The front door opens, and boots clomp against the wood floor as people enter the house. The footsteps get louder as I assume the people walk down the hall.

"How's she doing?"

Blake.

"Should we wake her up?"

Amos.

Wait... everyone has seen me snuggling up to Ryker this whole time?

My eyes widen as I sit up. Blake and his two boys along with Kieran stand on the other side of the couch. I try to tidy my clothes, but the wrinkles remain. My hand flies to my hair. It's probably a mess.

Ryker grunts and tugs on my arm. "Come back here."

I shove him and throw the blanket off me. "Ryker, there are people watching us."

When I try to stand, he grabs my hand.

He glances at the others. "Can you give us some privacy?"

They walk back outside, and Ryker maneuvers me so he can sit up. He pulls me sideways onto his lap and parks his hands on my outer hip.

I straighten my back, perching as far away from him as possible. "You're a little too enthusiastic for me. I think we should keep the PDA to a minimum when we're with people."

He leans forward and hovers his lips over mine. "And when we're not in front of people?"

My lips twitch against his as I fight my smile. "Not in the living room."

But when he tugs me closer, I relent and drape my arms around his neck.

He squeezes my hip. "You had me worried sick. Promise me you won't do something like this again."

"I was trying to help my mom. We need that money."

A breath hisses from between his teeth, and he shakes his head.

I scowl at him. "Don't be mad at me. I didn't know what else to do."

"Here's what you do—call me."

"I wasn't talking to you."

"Which was your choice."

"Because you didn't treat me right."

Ryker's lips curl into a lazy grin.

My nose scrunches. "Why are you smiling?"

"Because you're arguing with me."

"And that's funny?"

"No, but I realize the past couple times we've fought, you haven't been scared of me being angry with you."

I sift my fingers through the curls at the nape of his neck. "I'm a lot of things with you, but scared isn't one of them."

"Right back at ya."

His mouth captures mine, and I kiss him back. His hand clenches my hip as he deepens the kiss. I smile against his lips, loving the way he gives me all of himself. How he never holds back. How I can be myself and let go of my reservations when I'm with him.

He breaks away but rests his forehead on mine. His hand shifts to the side of my neck, and I lean into his touch. I ignore all my worries, my fears, and my problems. I push it all aside to spend a few more seconds with the guy who settles the turbulence around me. The guy who proves good men exist. The one who convinced me to take a chance on love.

The only guy who treats me like I'm his.

And shows me that he's mine.

He gives the side of my neck a small squeeze. "One more thing. Promise me you won't push me away again. I can't handle that."

I drag my fingers over his scruff. "I promise."

And with my promise, I cast aside all my rules, eager to start a life with the man I love.

CHAPTER 36

• • • • • • • • • •

Ryker:

Sharona's mom is getting discharged today. Opinions on her staying at the main house for a while?

Stephen:

Fine with me.

Kieran:

Are we just taking in everyone now?

Isobel:

Ignore the curmudgeon. This situation is acceptable to me.

Kieran:

You're talking like that on purpose. Stop.

Blake:

I'm fine with Marilyn staying on the farm. Would they share Sharona's room?

Ryker:

Probably. I didn't want to offer until I heard from y'all.

Kieran:

Are we all aware of the fact her mom will be going through withdrawal?

Ryker:

I'm aware. I'm prepared to help.

Blake:

The boys and I will help too.

Kieran:

Fine. Whatever.

Ryker:

Sharona says thanks. She also wants me to tell y'all they won't stay long.

Stephen:

Tell her she can stay as long as she wants.

Kieran:

I don't think you have any say in this since you don't live here.

Stephen:

She can stay with me if staying at the main house is a problem.

Kieran:

With you, a two-year-old, and your parents?

Ryker:

I'm not a fan of you smooth-talking my girl-friend, Santos.

Stephen:

<heart emoji>

Isobel:

<facepalm emoji>

CHAPTER 37

· · · · ● · ● · ● · ·

RYKER

As I lean against the threshold of Marilyn's hospital room, I watch Sharona with her mom and replay yesterday in my mind.

When I got Sharona's call, I about lost it. Lunch with the family came second place to protecting the woman I love.

I flew out of my mom and Cillian's house with Kieran on my heels. He texted everyone he could, and they all followed us to the address Sharona gave me. The door was unlocked, and one knock was the only warning I gave the lowlife threatening my woman before I entered the house.

I prayed to God for her to be safe and for me to find her.

And when I heard her voice, shrill like she was scared beyond reason, I took off. I stumbled into one of the rooms and found Jimmy with his arms around her.

My hand balls into a fist as I bring my focus back to my beautiful girl sitting next to her mom's hospital bed. She wanted to come to the hospital last night and introduce me to her mom, but I told her she needed rest after her ordeal.

Plus, I wanted to spend that time moving her back into the main house.

I wanted her back home.

Where she was safe.

Sharona waves her hand through the air as she tells her mom about the fall festival.

I met Marilyn this morning. After some quick introductions, Sharona told her what happened with Jimmy. When she reached the part where I showed up with the fam, her mother had looked at me like I was a goose who laid golden eggs.

Rare, valuable, and unfathomable.

Marilyn nods as she listens to Sharona, but her gaze slides to me. "Did you find out where the discharge papers are?"

Sharona turns to me, and her whole face brightens.

I walk over to them and drop my hand on the back of Sharona's chair. "The nurse said it would just be a few more minutes." I bend down to kiss my girl's cheek. "You good?"

She nods and stands. "Yep. I'm ready to get back home."

I wrap my arms around her but direct my attention to Marilyn. "My mom will be by the farm later with some clothes you can borrow."

We haven't gone back to Marilyn's house for her car or any of her things. We were able to give her an old sweatshirt and a pair of pants that belonged to Blake.

"She's bringing some other things for you too," I say. "When they get there, she and my stepdad will talk to you about that restraining order."

Marilyn and Sharona discussed getting one for Jimmy. My mom said she wanted to help, and Cillian got roped into it.

"Thank you," Marilyn says. "For everything. I'm sorry for putting you in this situation."

Without *this situation*, I wouldn't have Sharona, so I find it hard to complain. "We're happy to help."

Thirty minutes later, I'm driving the three of us to the farm. Marilyn talks nonstop from the passenger seat. Sharona sits in the middle of the bench seat and inserts a comment every now and then. I grab her hand and kiss the back of it. She softens into my side.

We drive down our lane, and I park the truck outside the main house. Marilyn hops out and shuts her door.

Sharona clutches my hand. "Are you sure it's okay if she stays with us?"

"Of course."

"It'll just be until we find our own place."

"It's fine. I already ran it past everyone." I climb out and hold the driver's side door open. "Let's get the introductions out of the way, so I can have you to myself."

She slides toward me. "Don't you have to work?"

"Took the day off."

She pauses, still perched on the driver's seat. "You took the day off for me?"

"Sure did."

Her eyes soften as she shifts forward in the seat. "I love that."

After I help her down, I wrap my arms around her and pull her closer.

She pushes on my chest and glances over her shoulder. "What are you doing?"

I sigh. "I was going in for a kiss. Thought it was obvious."

"My mom is right over there and waiting for us."

"So kiss me quickly."

She fights a smile. "Just one."

"Yes, ma'am."

She giggles, and I plant a kiss on her. The others walk toward my truck, so I step back and grab Sharona's hand, knowing she's still getting used to PDA. She introduces her mom to Isobel, Liv, Kieran, and Stephen before Blake joins us.

He removes his hat and shakes Marilyn's hand. "Good to see you're doing better."

"Thank you," she says. "I appreciate y'all letting me stay here for a bit. I'll help out in any way I can."

A black truck trundles down our lane and snags my attention.

"Genevieve said she wanted to stop by and check on Sharona," Blake says.

The brunette next to me gasps. "I completely forgot to fill her in on everything."

I frown as the truck stops a few feet from us. "She'll understand."

Both the driver and passenger side doors open. Genevieve jumps down from the passenger side, and climbing out of the driver's side is... Tex?

Kieran and I look at each other, and he shrugs.

Sharona nudges me. "What's going on with them?"

"No idea."

Genevieve rushes to her and crushes her in a tight hug. "I'm so glad you're okay. No more dangerous escapades, got it?"

Sharona pats her on the back. "I'll try."

Genevieve pulls back as Tex saunters over and stops next to her.

She grabs his hand but keeps her eyes on Sharona. "Are you okay? Do you need anything?"

Sharona's gaze shifts from their clasped hands to her friend. "No, I'm fine. Ryker's helped me a lot."

Tex clears his throat. "Gen told me what happened. I'm glad you're okay, Sharona."

Did he just call Genevieve Gen?

I look at Isobel to gauge her reaction. Not only is her dad holding hands with Genevieve—a woman much younger than him—but he has a nickname for her.

But Isobel is talking with Liv. The cousins hug, and Liv walks toward her car.

Stephen separates from the group and grabs her arm. "Where are you going?"

Kieran and Isobel walk off in their own conversation, and Sharona continues to talk with Genevieve and Tex.

I take a step away, my gaze stuck on Stephen and Liv. I want to know more about all the awkwardness between them lately.

Liv yanks her arm out of his grasp. "If you must know, I'm leaving."

"For the day?"

"For I don't know how long."

"What do you mean?"

"I'm thinking about leaving town and finding a new job. Taking a break from Mustang Cross."

By this time, all other conversations have stopped, and everyone watches them.

Stephen steps toward her. She lifts her hand as if to ward him off.

He crosses his arms. "Fine. Go ahead. It's not like we care anyway."

"I don't want you to care."

"We don't."

"Good."

"Great."

Liv stomps to her car and opens her door. She glances over her shoulder, and Stephen stares her down. With a final huff, she climbs into her car. She reverses and drives away, a dust cloud pluming behind her.

Sharona tugs on my sleeve. "What was that?"

My eyes shift to Stephen who marches toward the four-wheeler by the barn and takes off through the property.

To Genevieve and Tex walking hand-in-hand toward Isobel and Kieran.

To Sharona's mother taking a seat on the porch with Blake.

And I look to the brunette beside me. As new complications swirl through the lives around us, I run toward change. Toward my future and a family of my own.

I take Sharona into my arms. "That was life on Fable Farms."

EPILOGUE

· · · ● · ● ● · · ·

1 Year Later

RYKER

THE SUN LOWERS BEHIND the horizon while Sharona and I sit on the tailgate of my truck. Sweat beads beneath my shirt and slides down my back. I tug on my collar. It's not the warm October evening getting to me. It's thinking about what I plan to do in the next few minutes.

Sharona shifts next to me as a small pucker develops between her brows.

I grab her hand and thread my fingers through hers. "Something wrong?"

"I'm just thinking," she says.

"About?"

With her free hand, she swipes her fingers across her thigh as if she's drawing. I wait for her to come to me on her own time. Like she always does.

Her head snaps up. "I understand my mom wanting to take things slow, knowing her history with men, but it's been months. She's sober, has a job—she's improved so much. She loves Blake, and he's totally gone for her. He and the boys are family now. I don't know what either of them is waiting for."

"This is all new for her," I say. "Maybe she doesn't want to mess it up."

"Yeah, but if they're both in love, why can't they take that next step? She might have been scared at the beginning, but she's not anymore."

Why do I feel like we're not talking about Blake and her mom.

I envelop Sharona's hand in both of mine. "Maybe Blake's waiting to make sure your mom's ready."

She snorts. "She's ready. Believe me. There's nowhere else she'd rather be than here."

Now I know we're not talking about Marilyn. She's renting my childhood house from my grandparents and hasn't lived on the farm in months.

I squeeze Sharona's hand, trying to think of the perfect in to give her my gift.

She sighs. "Thanks for taking me out here. It's been a great birthday."

Bingo.

I reach into my pocket for the ring I grabbed before we left the house. "I have something for you."

That brings a small smile to her lips. "You already got me a cake. I have to thank Allegra for making it, by the way."

"You weren't a little disappointed I didn't get you anything else?"

"My gift was having a better birthday than last year. You don't have to give me anything. It's fine."

I shake my head and slide off the tailgate. "It's not fine, and of course, I had to get you something. I'm hoping to erase every bad birthday you've had, so I've got some work to do."

"That's a lot of pressure."

I sink down to the ground on one knee.

Her face crumbles. "Ryker." She covers her eyes with her hand.

I rub my knuckles against her calf and wait while she has a moment.

She sniffles and wipes the tears falling down her cheeks. "What are you doing?"

"Sharona, you are the most beautiful woman I've ever met."

A sob escapes her, and her brows draw together.

My hand skims down her calf, and I grip her ankle. "I love you so much. You are brave, strong, and kind. You slipped into my life when I didn't expect it, and you make me a better person. The only life I want is one where we get to grow old together."

She drops her head into her hands and cries even harder.

The crying is a good sign, right?

"Sharona? Baby?"

Her hands fall away... and she gives me a smile.

I exhale a breath and lift the ring between us. "Will you marry me?"

She nods. "Yes."

Both of our hands shake as I slip the ring on her finger. I get to my feet, cradle her face in my hands, and bring her mouth to mine. She kisses me back but breaks away a few times to catch her breath since she's crying.

I pull away and wipe her cheeks with my fingers.

She holds out her hand and stares at the ring. "It's beautiful."

"Good birthday so far?"

Her answering smile is wider than I've ever seen. "Yes." She places her palm on my cheek. "I love you."

I grip her wrist and place a kiss onto her palm. "I love you too. And I have one more present for you."

She laughs and shakes her head. "Ryker, I can't have another gift after this. I'm still processing."

"Well, prepare yourself because it's another big one."

Her smile fades. "Okay."

"But I need to show it to you."

She licks her lips. "You're scaring me."

I chuckle. "Would you trust me? Please?"

After helping her into the truck, I drive us through the property and some brush until we get to a clearing.

I park the truck and turn it off.

Sharona presses her lips together. "Okay... thank you?"

"Look in the back."

She shifts to her knees and faces the seat. "If it's a puppy, I told you, I wanted a bunny first."

I jostle her hip. "Get the roll of papers on the seat."

She rummages through the stuff behind me. "Got it." She plops back onto the seat with the papers in her hand. "Now what?"

"Open it."

She unrolls the papers. Stares at them, turns them, and drops them to her lap with a huff. "I'm sorry, but I have no idea what this is."

"They're floor plans."

"For?"

"For a house."

Her eyes widen and drift back to the papers. She's got it now.

When she looks at me again, the tears from before return. "You're building us a house?"

I squeeze her thigh. "I love the vote of confidence you have in me, but I'm not actually building it. I hired someone. It's the guy who built Cillian and my mom's house."

"We can wait. Until we have more money."

"Money's fine. And we're not waiting."

She grips my hand. "This is the best birthday ever. Thank you."

"Happy birthday, baby."

She leans forward, and I give her a kiss, ready to finish out her birthday.

Ready to start our life together.

Thank you for reading! I hope you enjoyed Ryker and Sharona's story. If you have the time, please consider leaving a review. Reviews help authors so much, and I would appreciate it.

Interested in what happens next with this sweet couple? Sign up for Karryn's newsletter and gain access to a free bonus scene. You'll also receive exclusive updates and more bonus content for Karryn's books.

Check out Karryn's website: KarrynOverstreet.com

ACKNOWLEDGMENTS

Thank you to everyone who helped me publish this book!

Always first, I need to thank my Father God in heaven for my ideas and for His guidance.

Thank you to my parents and my sister for their endless support and for always cheering me on in this journey.

To my beta readers, Leah, Michelle, and Kim, thank you for taking time out of your busy schedules to read my story. You provided me with valuable feedback and insight, and I so appreciate your help.

Debbie, thank you for editing this book for me. I'm so grateful for your feedback and encouragement.

A huge thank you to my prayer team for sending prayers my way.

Thank you to Alt 19 Creative for designing my cover. It is absolutely amazing, and I love the way you envisioned the main characters.

And thank you to all my readers. I hope you enjoyed Ryker and Sharona's story as much as I did!

About the Author

· · · ● · ● ● · · ·

Karryn Overstreet writes sweet romance stories with low angst and happy endings. Her books contain passionate kisses but no spice. She enjoys writing about young love and swoons when the main characters give their love interests nicknames. Karryn lives in south Texas on a few acres of farmland which is one of the inspirations for her stories.

ALSO BY KARRYN OVERSTREET

Christmas with the Loner: A Mustang Cross Novella (Kip and Allegra's story)

Chasing More: A Mustang Cross Novel (Cillian and Gwen's story)

Made in the USA
Middletown, DE
07 January 2026

24217882R00145